Petunia is in a doom and gloom ʜ
excitement of being Superman's
earth at Dockleaf with three chil
Spell 900) that she can't get rid of, and a phone that
doesn't ring. Where, oh where, is Otis B Henneberry?

But her luck is about to change. She inherits a castle!

Or *is* her luck about to change — for the worse.

From now on events move almost as fast as PP on her
skateboard.

Can Hiram H Hinkelheimer solve PP's cash flow
problem, and/or withstand assault by duck-headed
walking-stick?

Will Snivell, Snivell & Crouch v Phibbs, Argue &
Leech be the court-case of the century, or will the
baby-blue eyes of Bibi Babblecock-Browne, widow of
the late Lord Fruzey Few-Browne, Bt, melt the heart
of old Judge Poppadum?

Enter Vicky and Jassy in a starring role, and then
it's champers all round — until the dreaded *Merulius
Lacrymans* sneaks in through the cellar door.

Can the Antiques Roadshow (bring your old
antiques — and yourself — for valuation by Professor
Batty) save the day?

Your guess is as good as Furball's . . .

Terry Hassett Henry

The Witch
at
Batsford Castle

Illustrated by Terry Myler

THE CHILDREN'S PRESS

To Victoria and Chloe

First published 1991 by
The Children's Press
45 Palmerston Road, Dublin 6
Reprinted 1993

© Text Terry Hassett Henry 1991
© Illustrations The Children's Press

ISBN 0 947962 63 8

Typesetting by Computertype Limited.
Printed by Colour Books Limited, Dublin.

Contents

1

Dull Days in Dockleaf Cottage

The usual 'Wednesday afternoon picketeers' were out in force down by Dockleaf Cottage (home of the famous if eccentric Petunia Pennefeather and cat). Large signs bobbed up and down above the tangled weeds and bushes:

The rain began to pelt down so the local do-gooders headed for the shelter of the council pick-up and trundled back to the village, with loud mutterings of 'What's the use of trying to make a stupid witch see reason!!!'

Inside the cottage, Joey and Tansy put down the

binoculars and sighed in disappointment. (What a shame they weren't going to have the usual slanging-match!).

'It's so boring,' grumbled a voice from behind a pair of legs dangling over the side of a large and lumpy armchair. All the furniture in the cottage was large and lumpy and *none* of it matched 'accidently on purpose'. This was to give it, according to Petunia's interior designer, Monsieur Pidgeon, the 'Art Deco look'.

The children had long since decided that Monsieur could only have been a cross between a plumber who fancied himself as a furniture designer and a hawker in Mother Redcap's Market!

Tansy and her pal Joey looked towards the chair plonked in front of the glass doors. The glass was misting over as the cold rain dashed against it. Staring out, in the grumpiest of moods, was a young girl dressed in cropped jeans and a woolly sweater.

'Dull Days in Dockleaf Cottage . . .' Vicky continued to moan, squirting great clouds of *L'eau de gnat's eyebrow* in the air with total disregard for the witch's prized perfume.

Vicky, daughter of Sir Basil Ross-O'Brien, and two contemporaries from days of old had somehow ended up in the witch's cottage earlier that year. Inadvertently of course . . . because . . .

(a) They had been up to no good the day the bewitchment happened and . . .
(b) Old Petunia in her spell-making had made a 'pig's ear' of recipe 600!

(As explanations are *so* boring — to quote Vicky — for further details read *The Witch who couldn't*.)

'Joey,' hissed Vicky suddenly, legging it out of the chair. 'She's bombing up the pathway!'

'Get rid of the earrings, you idiot,' urged Tansy. Joey, who fancied the idea of wearing an earring, had been holding up some of the witch's vast collection for size and appearance.

'Tsk,' grumbled Joey. 'Just as I thought I'd found one to make me look dead-cool and interesting.'

'Dead-cool and interesting,' scoffed Vicky. 'The only time you've been interesting was that time the film reporter found sawdust on your shoulders and asked you if your brain was dripping.'

Tansy, ignoring the sparring pair, rushed to open the door in readiness for the arrival of Ms Petunia Pennefeather. A black-coated figure was whizzing up the pathway at breakneck speed, doing whirleys and wheeleys, ending her skateboarding antics with a side wobble at the doorstep.

'Quick, everyone look busy,' ordered Vicky. 'If she sees us idle again this week — she really will send us off to boarding-school.'

Tansy's freckles stood out in fright. Grabbing a clothes-brush from under a chair leg she began to thump large clouds of dust from any available piece of furniture within reach. She whisked furiously.

Joey, who was just after his eleventh birthday (not that birthdays meant a great deal to a lad who never seemed to get any smarter), gave a 'twang' here and there, rather half-heartedly, with a smelly old slipper.

Yanking the door open fully Tansy stumbled back on the marble bust of Napoleon Bonaparte, in use as a doorstep (the witch didn't keep ornaments just for looking at). A great gust of wind and rain blew in, followed by the witch clutching an outsize skateboard which almost filled the cottage.

'Shut the door, Batface,' she choked furiously, shaking off her cloak and flapping the wet skirts that hung about her bony legs.

'Joey!' she yelled loudly, busily unstrapping her knee-pads. 'Joey, clean my mode of transport at once. I don't want my wheels to seize up or end the day with dry-rust problems.'

'Your ladyship,' ventured Joey. The lad was none too fond of books and the translation of terms like 'mode of transport' did not readily spring to mind. 'You mean the skateboard?'

Now, old PP was not known for her wonderful patience and Joey had the great knack of shredding the few nerves she had to ribbons! Flopping herself into her basket chair, she growled, 'Don't know why

I ever allowed you lot to talk me into letting you stay, that time I made the wrong spell recipe! Think ...' she trilled. 'Think how happy I'd be if I'd got the recipe for miserable medicine correct — instead of letting you lot loose from some bewitchment ... And ...' she fumed, 'I'm sure you were up to no good then as now ... fume ... fume.'

The girls made tut-tutting noises about the weather and how wet the rain was and how windy the wind was and how misty the mist was (anything to change the subject). Vicky came in carrying an enamel basin of water with fresh herbs and a warm towel for the witch's sodden curls. She soothingly told PP to 'pop her feet in that', and she'd be none the worse for the soaking.

Grabbing the towel around her the witch flatly refused the water.

'Not on your nellie,' she scoffed. 'You *know* too much washing and water is bad for the skin — leads to wrinkles at an early age.' She scrutinised her feet with a pocket magnifying glass in case one of her 'pinkies' might have developed one due to wearing damp stockings. Stuffing the glass back in her pocket, she barked, 'Leave the water there and Furball can steam his fur up and improve his appearance!'

Furball, the little ball of salt-and-pepper fur who was the witch's cat, had crept in ahead of the dangerous hazard on the skateboard (PP), and headed straight for the wooden box by the antique stove in the kitchen. He had lived with PP for such a long time that neither of them could remember when he hadn't, so he was used to Petunia's rantings and ravings. He had thought of ESCAPE on many occasions — before the children had appeared. Since their arrival so many exciting things had happened that old Furball had actually come to enjoy pitting his wits against the witch. He and the children had, over the months, had many a hair-raising adventure.

Clattering her tea-tray as she quaffed her herbal tea, Petunia raged about her rival, Ivy ffrench-Fawcett. She was a jolly type of character and one of these people who always seemed to be in the right place at the right time... And worst of all, she was *clever*!!

'Does Miss Ivy have a good cause in mind?' asked Vicky with an innocent air. 'She's so kind, always raising money for indigent do-gooders and homeless cats and short-sighted dogs and things ... perhaps it's for a new roof in the ...'

'Hah!' scoffed the witch. 'It's for a new roof all right! The one *over* her head!!'

PP proceeded to imitate Ivy: ' "Pet-oonia, dear, I'm looking for a larger residence. Somewhere with character — landscaped gardens, a greenhouse, the odd loose box for a pony... I mean, Pet-oonia, one has to get out into the great outdoors. Commune with nature. No one lives in quaint little box houses anymore. Think green...!" Green what, may I ask? Frogs? Cucumber?? Pea soup??? Pig's liver????'

The children, desperately trying to keep serious faces, made sympathetic tcking-tcking noises.

'And then,' went on the distraught PP, 'then old Fiddle Face had the nerve to remind me how I used to live in such splendour before,' (her voice dropped to a whisper), 'the dratted poker game... When Uncle Oliver thought three aces were better than...'

'Miaow!' moaned Furball loudly, thinking he had better distract the witch at once, because if she began remembering the good old days — when the Penne-

feathers actually owned Creaky Hall in all its splendour
— life in the cottage would become unbearable.

'Hah! There you are, Hairbag!' snapped the witch.
(This was just one of the many loving terms she reserved
for poor old Furball.) 'And where,' she yelled like a
Sioux Indian, 'were you, Cat Hairs? In Creaky Hall?
When I needed you to make Ivy ffrench-Fawcett break
out in purple spots?' Furball never took his eyes off
the pointed-toed shoes — they had been known to
deliver many a whack aimed with the accuracy of a
heat-seeking-missile! 'You dumb dingbat, you. . .'

Joey came in, blathering about the evening paper's
arrival (anything in order to spare the cat from attack).
Witches enjoy the newspapers every *other* day as *no*
witch worth her salt believes for one minute that there
is enough news every day to fill every newspaper.
Luckily, this was the day for 'de paper'.

All was quiet for a while. The witch sat down to
digest the news. The children returned to the lumpy
armchairs and resumed dangling their legs over the
sides; grown-ups always complained about this but PP
never seemed to notice. Their faces stared gloomily
out of the rain-dashed windows.

Silence reigned — for at least five minutes. Then
Tansy whispered, 'I wish we could make another film
with Superman and old PP. It was such fun working
on the film set.'

'Even if we *were* only extras,' said Vicky. 'It was
great watching the witch outwit the real film stars. Her
part kept getting larger and most of theirs wound up
on the cutting-room floor.'

Joey giggled aloud. 'It makes my eyes water every
time I think of Otis B asking her "Did she study her
stuntwork in Hollywood?" It's a wonder,' he went

on, 'that no one ever found out that she couldn't fly. Remember the time when she pulled the inflatable balloon vest hidden in her cape and got the timing wrong and went Whack! into the poor unsuspecting cameraman... I wonder is he up and about yet?'

'Idiot!' yelled the girls, flinging cushions at him. 'Don't you know that CREATIVE STUNTWORK is what fills the seats!' imitating Otis B Henneberry's best Yankee drawl.

'Yes, siree!' they all chorused, holding imaginary fat cigars!

> *Make a Movie with Otis B*
> *His stuntwork makes*
> *MON...EY.*

'Silence,' roared the witch, whose concentration on the article *How to turn £100 into £1000 TAX-FREE in four days, five hours and twenty-five minutes?* had been fatally interrupted. 'This place is getting like a bear-garden. High time you were all sent to a proper school instead of idling about here, making a pig's ear of the decor ... just look at this, pools of water on the floor,' pointing to where she had stood while dripping her self dry, 'Clear it all up AT ONCE.'

Then suddenly she pointed her nose skywards and sniffed the air loudly. 'That is ... shouldn't there be the mouth-watering aroma of food from the kitchen, indicating a morsel of lunch for a poor witch consumed with a passion for the self-improvement of others?'

She buried her head in yet another book on *Flight Patterns: Some Difficulties Solved,* and the children retreated to the kitchen where they flung bits and pieces into saucepans, wondering if this was the day their fate was to be sealed. Boarding-school, with three references

to the subject in three days, seemed to be somewhat on the witch's mind these days.

Lunch was eaten in an atmosphere of gloom round the big old table, overshadowed by a great dresser loaded with lots of old plates and cracked bits of china (all carefully numbered, dated and put away 'for repair' — only of course nobody ever actually got round to repairing them.)

The kitchen resembled an old curiosity shop with endless clutter and bric-a-brac (which PP always referred to as 'her precious and valuable collection of *Objets d'Art*. On wet days, the children had great games of 'guess what' which sometimes lasted for hours (as when Joey had found the wellie warmers). Still, how boring to live in a house where everything actually had a purpose and a place of its own in a dull cupboard.

"Well, reely,' as the witch used to boast to anyone

who would listen, 'if the conversation at my table is ever dull — unlikely,' with a twitter, 'as this would be — at least the scenery is interesting. Observe this... Blaa ... Blaa ...'

'Now, sprats,' she began as lunch neared its end. 'About your education...'

The children let their cutlery fall with a clatter in shock, not daring to look at each other for fear the news might be too terrible.

'I've decided to...'

Before she could finish the sentence, Furball suddenly dashed from the boot box and took a flying leap over the table on to the window ledge. A motor-car was approaching, a motor-car that sounded as if it had whooping cough. There was only one person in the whole county of Ballyonder whose car sounded like that — the one and only Ivy ffrench-Fawcett (Petunia's rival in all things).

The children, delighted at the welcome interruption, rushed to the window to see a fine figure of a woman striding up the pathway with her usual gusto. Joey wrenched open the door in such a hurry that he almost fell into Ivy's ample bosom, smothering himself in layers of flowery fabric.

'Pet-oonia, dear...' began Ivy, in a voice that caused the still of the cottage living-room to boom with life. 'I've *got* to show you these builder's plans for my renovation of Hatter's Hall.'

Thrusting a sheaf of faintly inked drawings under the nose of the none-too-pleased Petunia, she sank herself (with great difficulty) into the best of the lumpy armchairs. Beaming at the children, she continued, 'Children! My! How you've grown...'

That kind of talk drove the children mad. 'What

does she expect us to do? Get smaller?' whispered Vicky. 'I used to think adults were brainy. Now I think their brains get soggy with age!' The other two gave silent giggles.

Ivy was in full voice. 'You must actually be feeding them, PP. Goodness knows, nobody thought they'd survive Dockleaf Cottage this length, ha, ha!'

Petunia scowled. 'Feeding them is not the problem — they've cultivated the art of living on practically nothing, like me — and a most valuable piece of learning that is. Everyone should acquire it,' looking at Ivy's curves. 'It's keeping them from cluttering up the place and making noise that is the problem,' she grumbled as she pretended to squint in a knowledgeable fashion at the drawings.

'Yes, indeed,' Ivy agreed. 'Perhaps it's time that they were sent away to. . .'

'Tea, anyone?' interrupted Vicky hastily. The last thing the children needed was not one but two people nattering on about the benefits of Discipline and Learning and Punctuality and Manners, etc. etc.

'Lovely,' beamed Ivy attacking a plate of cream cakes which Joey had just brought in. She obviously hadn't heard PP's aside about the advantages of living on air. 'Driving that old jalopy is such a challenge. I work up a jolly good appetite.' Munch, munch! 'Not that I'd be seen dead driving one of those newfangled Japanese things.'

Petunia pretended not to hear. She usually had trouble with anything even remotely mechanical. The last time she tried to make toast in the pop-up toaster the fire-brigade had to be called to hose down the side of the house. She had always avoided cars like the plague.

'Why annoy myself by actually buying one?' she had thought. 'Drat old Fiddleface!' She glared at her rival who was prattling on and on, in a most engaging way, full of new-house fever.

'And, of course, dry lining absolutely essential ... cavity walls no use ... damp-proof coursing must be checked ... double glazing a priority ... a dream kitchen — room for a double Aga, surrounded by endless copper pots and pans — walled gardens — red brick for growing peaches on a south-facing wall ... yak ... yak...'

'Of course,' parried Petunia. 'The trouble with a large house is...' She closed one eye as if reluctant to go on, though in fact, offhand, she couldn't think of anything.

'Is what?' barked Ivy.

Delighted to see that she had annoyed Ivy, PP appeared to ponder, finally coming up with, 'Large rooms are *so* hard to heat — all that hot air going up to the ceiling, leaving your feet stone cold. And the cost of heating oil!' She rolled her eyes to the low ceiling. 'And when there's a war, you can't get any...'

'Piffle and poppycock,' exploded Ivy. 'But of course you've got used to living in this shoe box. Not enough room to swing a cat anywhere.'

Furball slid further down into his box. He didn't like the turn the conversation was taking; it would be just like Ivy to arrange a demonstration.

Joey provided a welcome diversion by suddenly exclaiming, 'Miss Ivy! There's a robber trying to steal your car. I saw his head bob up a minute ago.'

'Are you sure? Where? Stand back!' shouted everyone at once. All eyes peered out of the dusty window towards the Morris 1000 car-cum-station-wagon parked askew at the gate.

A head of curly blond hair was bobbing about like a puppet on a string, apparently listening to some frenetic music on the radio.

'He's not in much of a hurry for a robber,' said Joe. 'Look, he's even checking that the radio works before he'll take it.'

'Probably can't get it to start,' said Vicky.

Ivy, having finally managed to locate her glasses, said, 'How silly of me! In all my excitement I forgot Jassy was with me.'

'Jassy?' asked everyone. No one had ever heard of Jassy before.

'My sister Drusilla's boy — she's not been in the best of health recently and she's taken herself off to one of those health spas, in Baden Baden or Vichy or Marienbad or somewhere ... won't be back until spring.' Then looking at PP with her best 'must-do-one-good-deed-a-day' face she whispered, 'One cannot refuse a child a home. Indeed, you know all about that yourself. As I always say, you're an inspiration to us all, taking *all* these children into your teeny-weeny little cottage.'

'That,' scowled the witch, 'isn't exactly what I had planned. What happened was...'

'Can we invite him in?' asked Tansy hopefully, anxious both to circumvent Petunia on the subject of schools and meet Jassy.

'Well, just for a moment — I really must dash — got to catch the builder before he starts ripping the place apart!'

A tall boy in sensible clothes — grey flannels, checked shirt, home-knitted sweater — appeared at the door, mumbling through a brace on his teeth, 'Yiss, Aunt Ivy.'

'Jassy, come and meet my oldest school pal, Petunia Pennefeather, and her...' She was at a loss how to describe them.

'Friends,' smoothed Vicky. 'And this is our pet cat, Furball,' prising him out of the boot box.

Petunia was looking aghast. 'Another dratted child on the horizon. If I've said it once, I've said it a thousand times — children don't come in small doses. They attract other children from out of the woodwork and before you know where you are they're all over the place. Disgusting little germs. There should be a chemical to get rid of them... Well, that's one problem I'm not going to have come September.'

'What's happening in September?' asked Ivy, pulling on her four-button gloves.

'They're going to be sent away to school,' shouted PP. 'That's what's going to happen. Teach them a thing or two ... and take them out of my hair. Six weeks more and they'll all be gone ... and I'll have the place to myself again. Nothing but peace and quiet. I'll be able to hear myself think.'

'But Pet-oonia dear,' soothed Ivy, unbuttoning her gloves. 'Remember your blood pressure. There's nothing to get excited about. But have you thought of...'

'Of what,' snapped Petunia.

'Of the cost, of course.' Ivy's voiced dripped sympathy. 'You lead such a sheltered life in your little cottage, away from it all. But have you any idea of just what it costs to send children away to school these days? Thousands, literally thousands. And that's just for starters...'

Ivy was warming to her theme; it didn't suit her plans at all to have the children sent away just when she had Jassy on her hands; with a skilful bit of manoeuvering she was confident that Jassy would, in fact, spend most of his time at Dockleaf. She certainly didn't want him on the loose in her newly decorated Hatter's Hall. 'There are all those extras. Swimming lessons, tennis lessons, gym, bacon for breakfast, library subscriptions, riding lessons, fencing gear, theatrical make-up...'

'Theatrical make-up,' croaked PP.

'For end-of-term theatricals, of course. I'm afraid it's not like the old days when school fees covered everything. Now they just buy you the bare essentials ... and those extras can *double* your initial outlay ... which, of course, will be in the region of ... say, three to four thousand apiece...'

'Three or four ... thousand...' Petunia sank into a chair.

'Twelve thousand for three,' went on Ivy briskly, being a good hand at the maths, especially simple arithmetic. 'Just add on those extras and you get...'

'Don't,' moaned PP.

'I believe that in some schools,' and Ivy's voice sank to a whisper, 'pupils are required to bring their own computer with them. And you know what *they* cost.'

'Computers?' PP had a glazed look in her eyes.

'And — I know this will come as a shock to you, dear Pet-oonia — the worst thing about boarding-schools these days is that they only take the children off your hands for *days* at a time. What between half-term, and days off, and letting them home every other week-end ... why, you're lucky if you get rid of them for fifteen days out of the thirty. Not that, of course, you want to get *rid* of them. You're only thinking of their good. But is it worth it? That's what you must ask yourself, dear Pet-oonia. Balance all the money you'll be out against the knowledge that by keeping them at home you're giving them the benefit of loving care and attention at all times — not to mention help with their homework which they *never* get at school.'

Rebuttoning her gloves, she summoned Jassy, twittering, 'Must dash. Walls going up. Walls coming down.'

'And that,' whispered Vicky to Tansy as she closed the door behind Ivy, 'is, I think, the end of that.'

Schoolwork

2
Halloween — in July

As Ivy had so shrewdly calculated, Jassy spent most of his time at Dockleaf Cottage. But as the children were careful to keep him out of sight and Ivy provided him with what Joey called 'toad grub' (i.e. egg sandwiches) for his lunch, PP remained in blissful ignorance that yet another sprat was lurking in the undergrowth. So Jassy had a ball, exploring with the children, sussing out the tree-house and the old bicycle shed (which PP described as her 'hanger for light aircraft' and which, the children explained to him, contained all the broomsticks on which she had crash-landed on account of not being able to fly).

She only set eyes on Jassy once, the time she had floated down out of the sprawling branches of her treasured judas tree, binoculars slung about her neck, riding in what appeared to be a half-filled hot-air balloon; she had been checking for the usual Wednesday picketeers. Letting it over the side of the basket, she glared at Jassy who had fallen over in fright at this sudden apparition.

'What are you doing here?' she scowled at him. 'Begone! And beware! It isn't safe to be round here. Qualified personnel only. Got it?' Which, as she had booby-trapped the lane for the picketeers, was fair warning. However, as Jassy always came in over the fence, it was superfluous in his case.

'Got what?' he quavered, as PP disappeared.

'Never mind,' advised Vicky, coming out from behind

a bush. 'She's just in one of her MYOB moods.'

'Mind Your Own Business,' explained Tansy.

Petunia bounded up the path and into the cottage. She was sick to the teeth of the locals coming down every week declaring her property an eyesore. 'Indeed,' she muttered, as she leafed through her press cuttings (her favourite relaxation), 'if they or their old cronies had been in a Hollywood movie they would be making Knockaleen into a museum — tribute to a great star — but just because old PP is star material, they're green with envy. But I'll fix them.'

Reaching for the phone, she called Nutgrove Studios to see if anyone had offered to back her next movie, only to be told that Otis B Henneberry was out.

'Seeking a new location, no doubt,' thought the witch, thinking that the roar of the crowd and the luxury of a penthouse suite were not far away. She blew the dust off his framed photograph and settled down for a nap with cold tea-bags on her eyelids, as recommended in *Showbiz Weekly* for the refreshment of tired eyes. 'Wouldn't anyone's eyes be tired looking at children all the time? . . . and if I catch that Jassy again. . . I'll. . .'

Zzzz . . . Zzzzz . . . Zzzzzz. . .

A blood-curdling set of yells from the laneway roused her from a pleasant dream in which she was just stepping up to accept an Oscar for the Best Supporting Actress.

'Agglll . . . Waell. . .' More yells and loud bawling of 'Help, I've been attacked. . .I've been blown up by a nuclear bomb. . . I'm half dead and I haven't had time to make a will. . .'

The children and Jassy rushed from the garden to see what had bombed the quietest lane in Knockaleen. What a sight! A fat body, wearing voluminous knickers was lying, legs up in the air, at the bottom of a great hole, half filled with flour, which someone had carefully dug right outside the gate to Dockleaf Cottage. They reached down to haul the injured party out ... and discovered that the person underneath the layers of flour and flowery underwear was none other than Ivy ffrench-Fawcett!

PP stayed indoors, waiting to hear which particular do-gooder had fallen victim to her fiendishly clever trap. When Ivy, supported by Jassy and Vicky, was helped in, she could hardly suppress a snigger. She had to turn aside several times, in between complaining about flour dust on the furniture, to hide a smirk.

Joey poured a good dollop of cooking sherry into a teacup for poor shell-shocked Ivy and everyone waited for her to explain what had happened.

'I was ... I was...' she faltered, in between trying to remember what had happened and wondering at the odd taste of the tea. 'I was just coming to tell you about my little brainwave for my Halloween party...' She dissolved into tears for fear that she might have suffered irreversible brain damage. 'Boo, hoo. Who could have done such a thing to a poor little woman like me?'

Just then the do-gooders, having heard the explosion, arrived on the scene and PP shot out through the front door and invited them in to see the trouble they had caused. Mrs Daphne Furey declared it had *nothing* to do with the local committee, and everything to do with the fact that Dockleaf Lane was a hazard to all.

PP declared that their pick-up had weakened the road surface and that all that pounding up and down with heavy placards had turned pint-sized potholes into huge craters. Relentlessly pressing home a point on the dangers of crowd control, she ended on a ominous note.

'Perhaps Ivy should sue them for bodily injuries. Not just one! *All* of them should be joined in the action!'

When the locals heard the word 'sue' and got a few more earfuls of legal phraseology, they were off like scalded cats and rushed down the road, vowing never to return. PP went back to the cottage, well pleased with herself and her afternoon's work.

'It's a Halloween party, next week,' explained Vicky. 'Isn't it a great idea?'

'Halloween in July,' scoffed the witch. 'What bird-brain thought that one up?'

'Aunt Ivy did,' said Jassy helpfully.

Ivy was gradually coming round (after four cups of Joey's tea) and declared through a floury haze that it wasn't against the law to hold a Halloween party in July. 'I mean, the weather is always freezing in October and everyone gets soaked tricking and treating. So doesn't it make the most marvellous sense to hold it in the summer.'

Which, when everyone thought about it, seemed a very good idea indeed.

'Besides,' soothed Vicky as she helped the still shaken Ivy to her feet. 'It will be a wonderful opportunity for us to see your new renovations at Hatter's Hall.'

'Mad Hatter's Hall,' twittered PP to Furball, who was the only one listening.

Ivy's eyes brightened and, clutching her flour-filled basket and supported by Jassy, she set off with shaky steps for home, convinced that walking should come with a health warning.

'Keep fit, my elbow,' she muttered. She'd definitely motor everywhere from now on...

The night of the Halloween party was clear and calm.

Everyone got dressed up except PP, who went as herself, in a Paris designer gown she had fancied since the film *première* (available at a discount, since nobody else had the broomstick figure to fit into it.)

The girls had chosen to go as rock stars and the boys as Roman warriors, draped in the best of old PP's hot-press. Even Furball wore a cat-burglar vest and a black sock over his face.

As they made their way there, PP moaned about having to attend at all. 'But I must go,' she sighed. 'Otherwise she'd say I'm as sick as a parrot over her newly decorated mansion.'

'Oh, indeed she might,' agreed the children, secretly dying to get to one of Ivy's famous parties.

'Not, of course,' continued the witch, 'that I, Petunia Pennefeather, give a hoot whether she lives in a mansion or a matchbox. Insufferable woman ... full of the joys of spring morning, noon and night, winter and summer ... mutter ... mutter... What I wouldn't give to knock her grand ideas! Hatter's Hall, indeed. Mad Hatter's Hall, more likely ... nag ... nag...'

The lights of Hatter's Hall shone brightly. The house and long gardens looked wonderful as the children approached the curving stone steps leading up a doorway which had begun life in a Gothic castle in Scotland. Judging from the number of cars around, it seemed that almost every inhabitant of Knockaleen was at Ivy's special Halloween party.

Ivy appeared, dressed as Cleopatra, with a long, black, straight-haired wig and a rather odd-looking snake draped about her neck and person. As she noticed everyone backing away, she declared that it was perfectly house-trained.

Nobody dared to ask what she meant.

'House-trained? Cats are house animals,' thought Furball, deciding to give the asp a wide berth.

'Children, Pet-oonia dear. How nice to see you! Do come in. Make yourselves at home and help yourselves to the buffet,' she ordered good-heartedly.

Just as PP was about to attack the punch-bowl with gusto, Ivy elbowed her out of the room, declaring that she must see the Adam fireplace in the Blue Drawing-Room.

'The chairs are walnut,' she explained to Petunia and the admiring throng that had gathered in her wake. 'Cartouche-shaped padded backs. Cabriole legs. Scrolled feet. Louis Quinze. . .'

'Cans what?' asked PP, a remark that threw a portly young man in the crowd into ecstasies of admiration.

By now they were in the Green Drawing-Room.

'I'm sure you'll be interested in this,' simpered Ivy, drawing attention to a small piece of furniture. 'A *bonheur-de-jour*. Kingwood and parquetry. Applied with gilt-metal mounts. On fluted turned tapering legs, with sabots. Said to be,' here her voice dropped to a whisper, 'from the salon of Maria Antoinette. Louis Seize.'

'Says? What does Louis say? Pray tell us.'

'What wit!' said the portly young man. 'What rapartee!'

'And observe these chairs. Original tapestry covering. The fables of La Fontaine.' Peering closely at the faded and frayed uphostery, she said, 'I think this one is the fox and the goose. . .'

'One born every day,' murmured PP.

'. . . from the chateau of St Cloud.'

'San clue! Hasn't got a clue. Poor Ivy. . .'

'And on this canape here, you can see. . .'

'Canapé. Did I hear someone say "canapé"? Reminds me I'm starving!'

With the young man still in rapt attendance, Vicky dragged PP away, hissing, 'It's all French. Don't show your ignorance.'

'French? If you ask me more like double dutch. Lead on to the canapés. . .'

After supper in the Regency Salon du Thé, Ivy waved the head of the snake around, declaring that it was time for a spot of culture.

'Hands together for that well-known conductor, Mr O'Boom,' cooed Ivy.

Up got Mr O'Boom and began conducting furiously.

'He's murdering Vivaldi,' scoffed PP, who had heard it all before (at the local hairdresser) and could la-de-da a few bars ahead of the posse.

Everyone else listened carefully and gazed at the conductor as if he had written it all himself.

'Why does everyone look like they'd swallowed a slice

of lemon?' whispered Joey.

'This is Art!' said Vickey severely. 'You're not meant to enjoy yourself. Look solemn . . . and pained.'

'A knowledge of music is *so* important these days,' gushed Ivy. 'We must all put our best foot forward for the European Year of Culture.'

'Best foot?' repeated PP. 'Splendid idea. Let the dancing begin.' Rushing up to the bandstand, where Mr O'Boom had just been about to commence the world *première* of his Sycophantic Variations on two notes in four keys in as many movements as the audience would remain seated for, she ordered him to play something 'with a bit of jizz in it'.

Petunia insisted that the boys each gave her a dance and she and Jassy opened the ball. But Joey declared he's rather die than have her tread on his toes. Actually he was more afraid of what might happen if *he* stepped on *her* toes — which, as dancing had not been taught in his formative years (as a stable-boy) was more than likely. He grabbed a tray of hors-d'oeuvres and began to circulate among the guests. The girls were despatched to track him down as PP had no intention of being a wallflower, especially in her Dior Sans Laurent.

Luckily help was at hand, in the person of the fat youth who had been following them around on the house tour. Tansy accidentally knocked a glass of punch over him, and full of apologies the girls offered to refill his glass and mop his suit.

'No need, girls,' he chuckled, introducing himself as Desmond Snivell. 'Just tell me who is that ravishing creature you were talking to just now? When Miss ffrench-Fawcett was showing us her charming house. You must be a friend of hers.'

'Friend?' asked Vicky, puzzled.

'That radiant creature in the pink sequins.' Following his enraptured gaze, the girls' eyes fell upon Petunia.

'You mean Pet. . .'

At that precise moment PP rounded on them. 'Pests! Haven't you found that flibbertigibbet Joey yet? Call yourselves. . .'

'Ouch. . .' ouched Vicky, as PP's fingers dug into her arm. Then pushing forward the fat youth, she went on, 'Meet Mr. . .'

'Desmond Snivell,' said the youth, bowing.

'Ms Petunia Pennefeather,' supplied Tansy.

'Tell him, late of Creaky Hall and Demense,' whispered PP. 'Property of a gentlewoman lately removed from the country and shortly to be offered for sale in two lots.'

Seeing Tansy's mouth drop open, she continued, 'Mustn't let him think I'm a common or garden type of person.'

Mr Snivell gasped in amazement; he seemed about to say something, but only a strangled sound emerged. The girls thought that this must be how love at first sight affects one and watched the process with interest.

'Well, are you going to ask me to dance, or are you going to stand there with your mouth open catching flies?' snapped PP.

She grabbed poor Snivell by the arm and they tottered out on to the dance floor. As the band was playing a rumba they strutted about like a pair of angry peacocks, with PP throwing herself into the dance with gusto. She'd show Ivy ffrench-Fawcett she could dance, even if she didn't know her quinzes from her seizes.

The rest of the guests looked on in great amazement. Old PP, the recluse from the end of the lane, had somehow, over the last year, become this sophisticated

Hollywood star complete with fame and fortune, not to mention a ready-made family, and was now the star of the dance floor.

'Let me guess what you do,' prattled dear Desmond, as they cha-cha'd. After the initial shock of finding himself doing an exhibition dance he was enjoying himself; relentlessly ground down by a doting mother and a pair of uncles left over from the last century, he was never allowed out on his own (he had only made it to the party by purloining the invitation sent to his Uncle Snivell). 'Obviously you're a successful career woman. In what particular — and judging by your ensemble . . . lucrative — field, do you dabble?'

PP smiled enigmatically and redoubled her cha-chaing.

'That name . . . Pennefeather,' queried Snivell when they met again on an eyeball to eyeball basis. 'Rings a bell. Let me ask you . . . father's name . . . mother's name . . . place of birth . . . date of birth. . .'

PP supplied the information to the first three questions, coyly responding 'Over 21' to the fourth.

'Grotesque,' said Desmond. 'Unbelieveable. Bizarre. Unprecedented. I can't believe my ears!'

'If you can't believe your own ears, who will?' riposted PP, taking time out to do a pirouette and a fandango.

When she met up with the gasping Desmond again, he was now holding a brief-case, hastily fetched from his uncle's BMW.

Grabbing the nearest microphone, he called for silence and after a dramatic pause announced:

'Ladies and gentlemen . . . and children . . .' ('What's he got against cats?' thought Furball.) 'Allow me to introduce Ms Petunia Pennefeather. This ravishing

creature on my arm is none other than the missing link in the Pennefeather/Few-Browne inheritance. Ms Petunia Pennefeather is the niece of Fruzey Few-Browne ... *Lord* Fruzey Few-Browne!'

You could have heard a pin drop in the Louis Quinze drawing-room as everyone reacted to the news.

'Lord Few-Browne,' croaked Ivy, sinking heavily into a spindly-legged chair (it would never be the same again).

'I would now ask the interested parties to withdraw next door to hear me read a document of great importance.'

Naturally everyone followed him and the crowd was soon wall-to-wall in the Louis Philippe morning-room. The children made sure of ringside seats and Furball slipped through a sea of legs to join Petunia, who had been escorted into the room by young Snivell and was now seated in a rare William IV rosewood *fauteuil de bureau,* with padded U-shaped seat, on turned and reeded legs, the pride and joy of Ivy's collection; the latter's left eye was twitching madly at the thought of the wear and tear on her treasure.

Rooting in his bag for what seemed like ages, young Snivell began to read a yellowed document, which he had been entrusted with that very afternoon to bring direct to his firm's safe-deposit box in the bank. And which naturally, his attention having been distracted by a beautiful blonde in a red sports car, he had neglected to do, intending to remedy the omission in the morning.

Drawing himself up to his full 5 foot 6 inches height, he began in the solemn tone of voice reserved for reading wills and foreclosing mortgages:

TO WHOM IT MAY CONCERN

'Bashford Castle: The 21st day of November, 1981. I, Sir Lord Few-Browne, being of sound mind and body, this day make my last Will and Testament. To my dear wife, who tried hard to spend every penny I ever had, I leave one penny!' Pause, while everyone gasped; a few of the more frivolous twittered Ha! Ha!' 'To my true friends and servants I leave the sum of two thousand pounds.' (More gasps, this time of envy). 'The bulk of my estate, my castle and all its lands, I leave to my next-of-kin, my greatnieces, Tallulah and Petunia Pennefeather of Creaky Hall.

'Dated this day,
Fruzey, Lord Few-Browne of Bashford.'

Silence filled the room and all eyes were turned towards PP. Mistaking her silence for shock, young Snivell ordered someone to get her a brandy.

PP waved it away and asked sweetly if all that meant

that she really owned a castle.

Snivell nodded and smiled.

'And land?' continued PP, even more sweetly.

Again young Snivell nodded and smiled.

'For over ten years, at least?'

More nods and smiles.

'Then why,' roared PP, leaping to her feet, 'hasn't anyone bothered to tell me!'

Snivell paled and collapsed into a chair. For the first time it struck him that the reading of the will might not have been the right thing to do. How would he explain all this to his uncle, no doubt, at this very moment, sleeping peacefully in the knowledge that the will was deep in the bowels of the bank?

'Speak up!' commanded PP, but all poor Snivell could do was mumble about the 'difficulty of obtaining whereabouts . . . land searches . . . negative response . . . proving title . . . etc. etc. . . .'

At this precise point in time, the older Snivell, uncle of the impressionable Desmond, and senior partner in Snivell, Snivell & Crouch, materialised. He had come, not to attend the party (he never went to parties) but to retrieve his BMW which was not allowed out late at night.

'Silly boy,' he hissed at his nephew (who was being relieved of the brief-case and rushed from the room by a faithful retainer of the firm), in a voice that had icicles dangling from it, 'I'll see you in the morning.'

Bowing low, he addressed Petunia: 'Perhaps you would call into the office at your convenience and we will discuss the matter.' As Petunia began to speak, he held up a hand and said in a voice which still had a few icicles lurking around the edges, 'Now, now. I never mix business and. . .' he looked around at the motley fancy-dress revellers, '... pleasure.' So saying, he swept from the room.

As the guests returned to the dancing, Ivy's face was a picture. Her cheeks were bright red and the snake looked like it had died of shock.

'What a night!' thought Vicky.

'A castle!' said Tansy.

'Land,' whispered Joey. 'Bound to be a few horses around.'

'What luck!' thought Jassy enviously.

Aware that the night's events had wiped the smug smile, if not the jolly grin, from the face of old Fiddleface, Petunia extended a limp hand and gushed her thanks for 'the most wonderful evening of my life'. Then briskly, she ordered, 'Come along, children. We must dash. So many things to attend to. A castle and demense. Responsibilities. Tenants. Stables. Lands in escrow...' Meeting her hostess's gaping stare, she inclined her head half an inch. 'And, again, thanks for a lovely *little* party...'

'Ivy looked like a gannet that had swallowed a whale!' giggled the children on the way home. 'A castle ... we're all going to live in a castle...'

The two senior partners of Snivell, Snivell & Crouch, reviewed in silence, over comforting cups of cocoa, the calamity that had befallen them. Never ones to bandy words about lightly, it was some time before either of them spoke.

'Comes of sending a goose on a boy's errand,' concluded the less senior Snivell.

'We'll play the Number One Card,' decided the senior Snivell; he boasted that he had a trick for every trade.

3

The Trouble with Castles

The children couldn't wait for Jassy to arrive next morning.

'Didn't we tell you? Something out of the ordinary always happens to old PP!'

'Great for you,' mumbled a forlorn Jassy. 'You're all going to live in a castle. But what about me? I'll have to stay in Mad Hatter's Hall, with misery guts Ivy.'

'Oh, but you'll have to come,' wailed Joey. 'I'm sick of being surrounded by women.'

'Say that again,' warned the girls, 'and ... we'll...'

The air was full of argument, which was only quelled by a scream from the witch. She was in irritable mood and wasn't about to put up with noise from a pack of unruly children. The truth was that in the cold light of morning she was beginning to have second thoughts about the castle.

'Castles? Castles! Did I ever say I wanted a castle? Goodness knows what it's full of. Woodworm. Dry-rot. Cobwebs. Ghosts. Probably went to rack and ruin in old Greatuncle Fruzey's time and been unlived in ever since. Most castles are only a pain in the neck. A drain on the pocket. Might as well dig a hole in the ground and throw the money into it. Blah, blah, mutter, mutter...'

The children realised that if they wanted to know more about the castle, they would have to proceed carefully.

'Where exactly is it?' asked Vicky in her most winning voice. 'Perhaps it's too far away and can't be reached without a search-party.'

'Worse luck,' scoffed PP. 'It only happens to be in the next county, dratted thing.'

'Brilliant!' shouted Joey and Tansy. 'When can we go?'

The witch drew herself up to her full height (which was not very much but it was all she had), pointed her chin and growled, 'We? We're not going to any castle. Not now! Not then! Not ever! And if I hear another mouthful with the word "castle" in it, I'll...' she snarled viciously.

That little outburst put everyone in the doldrums. They had so been looking forward to living in a castle.

Ivy's arrival coincided with all this doom and gloom. Entering the kitchen where great black clouds of disappointment hung in the air like incense, she requisitioned a cup of tea and a bun, while throwing a quick 'refresher' look at her hastily written notes. She was not about to be outsmarted by old PP and her crumby inheritance.

'Pet-oonia, dear,' she began. 'Have you given any more thought to your *wonderful* inheritance? I know you will be able to deal with the dry-rot, the leaky roof, the wet-rot, the mildew on the walls. Tee, tee...' she twittered. 'And, of course, they have wonderful chemicals nowadays for combating cockroaches and swarms of death-watch beetles. And it's really quite safe — when you wear the protective clothing...' she continued, waiting to see PP's face register shock and horror.

Petunia didn't bat an eyelid. She knew all there was

to know about derelict old buildings. The trouble with. The upkeep of.

If Ivy was disappointed at this lack of reaction, she didn't allow it to show. This was a battle of wits and she couldn't lose face.

Finishing the iced bun she was ceremoniously dipping into her tea like an ancient rite, she played her trump card.

'Oh, and taxes,' she purred. 'You must let me recommend my accountants. You'll need them to help and advise you on what investments to cash in ... when you have to pay...' and here her voice became practically inaudible, 'Residential Property Tax.'

The word 'tax' was guaranteed to send PP into a mad rage at the best of time. And this wasn't the best of times.

'Tax!' she croaked hoarsely. 'Why would I have to pay tax on a heap of rubble I don't even want?'

'A silly law. I've always thought so myself,' agreed Ivy, delighted to find she had scored a bull's eye. Obligingly she filled in a few details: 'Value over £250,000, payment at 6% per annum, rising to 10% in leap years. Adjustment for the over-55s — should apply to you, dear — of 5% or £5,000, whichever is the lesser. All property to be aggregated, so they'll add the value of Dockleaf to the castle. And you've no idea of what quaint little cottages like this are fetching at the moment. These people — yuppies, I think they call them — have an insatiable appetite for places like this. They move in and do them up from top to toe. Why, I heard the other day of a couple. . .'

PP, who had been listening to all this with a face frozen into thunderstruckness, suddenly leapt to her feet.

'STOP!' she screamed. 'Enough of this nonsense! There won't be any tax. . . I'm not going to live there.'

'Immaterial, my dear Pet-oonia,' simpered Ivy. 'If you're the owner you have to pay.'

'But there may not be a castle at all,' put in Vicky. 'We won't know until we've checked it out.'

'It's in the phone book,' pressed Ivy relentlessly. 'I looked it up.'

'That means nothing,' said Vicky. 'Could be a total wreck — with a gatelodge.'

PP paused in mid-scream. The whole subject was getting her down.

'The only way out, it seems to me,' Ivy's voice was oh-so-helpful, 'might be the will. I mean if it wasn't valid. Then the castle wouldn't belong to you at all.'

Secretly she was dying to know how PP had got on with Snivell, Snivell & Crouch; she had heard, via the Knockaleen exchange, that PP had put through innumerable calls to their office in Drimaleen, but hadn't been able to find out what had happened.

Now, putting the witch's ill-temper and her waving away of a castle together, she was fast coming to the conclusion that maybe PP hadn't inherited anything. Or maybe a codicil lopped off the Pennefeathers with a farthing. Delighted, she helped herself to another bun.

The truth was that PP hadn't had much luck with Snivell, Snivell & Crouch. The will seemed to be in order — the payment of a small fee, handed over with much reluctance, assured her that she was, indeed, the rightful heir of Fruzey Few-Browne and the owner of Bashford Castle — but that was all the progress she had made.

When she had phoned the dashing young Desmond Snivell the morning after the party he wasn't available; had just taken a holiday on the Trans-Siberian Express, calling at every trouble spot in the Middle and Far East, a holiday that would last months, if not years. Snivell Senior was also unavailable; gout, gum disease and housemaid's knee had taken their toll of one who, though physically strong to the outward eye, was constitutionally as weak as an undernourished reed. The second Mr. Snivell was laid low with a mystery virus and was not expected back, if at all, for several months. As for Mr. Crouch, he was only a name on the fascia board, having departed the scene in the early days of the century.

When PP recollected her scattered wits, Vicky was saying to Ivy, 'We really can't come to any decision until we've seen the place.'

PP looked at her thoughtfully. The dingbat had a point. The sooner they saw the place the better. Then she could sell it or knock it down, and get back to more important things like resuming her film career.

'And if it is half-derelict,' said Ivy, 'just remember that if you take the roof off they can't tax you. If I were you I would consider it as a matter of urgency. Because you know, of course, that you will be taxed on owning it from the day you inherited it.'

'That settles it,' roared PP. 'We'll go west immediately. Me and Vicky and Tansy.' She looked at poor Joey grudgingly. 'And you. We'll need you to take off the roof.'

'I'd be very happy to give you a lift,' cooed Ivy. 'Jassy and I were thinking of a few days' holiday.'

'Who said anything about you? I'm certainly not having *you* and that whipper-snapper along.'

'But just think, dear, of what it's going to cost you. The railways have got *so* expensive. Why the fare to Clashash is £34.06 for an adult and £22.67 for persons under twelve.'

'We'll only need singles,' croaked PP.

'But of course, dear. The single is £33.88 and £20.46. Add taxis to the station — say £10.87 — and Heavens knows how much it will cost to get to your castle from Clashash station — another £54.79 I shouldn't wonder.'

PP, who was pretty nimble at the old mental maths and had come up with a figure not far short of £200, suddenly broke out into a great big smile that shot the doom and gloom to kingdom come.

'Why, of course! On mature reflection, what a splendid idea!' Shaking Ivy warmly by the hand, she went on, 'I wouldn't dream of setting the old tootsies on the ancestral soil without having you, my oldest friend, by my side.

'As for your offer of a lift, this would be the *least* consideration in my mind, though I'll quite understand if you don't want to leave your car behind – some half-crazed idiot might try and steal it. And Jassy will be *such* a help with the roof. Right then, that's settled. We leave at the end of the week. Thursday, 9 am. Sharp.'

As she swept away, the children heard her singing to herself in an assortment of tunes: *Any port in a storm. Save the pence and don't spend the pounds. Never look a gift horse in the mouth – spare yourself the sight of old Ivy's molars. A pound in the pocket is worth two at the ticket-office. All that glisters is pure gold.*

Furball emerged from a refreshing nap to the sound of cheers and shouts.

'We're going to live in a castle,' whispered Tansy. 'Isn't it exciting!'

'I'll take a raincheck on it,' thought Furball. 'I know this is all going to be a Terrible Experience.'

4

Bashford Castle

At last the great day arrived. Everybody was breathless with effort. The girls had collected wellies and warm coats, tinned food and woollen blankets. The boys weighed in with crates full of old comics, candles, paraffin lamps, torches. Petunia had spent the time briefing herself on validity of title, obligations of executors, malpractice (of solicitors), grounds for sueing malpracticing solicitors, and sundry other matters, having decided, now that she had a car, to call to the offices of Snivell, Snivell & Crouch en route, give them a piece of her mind and ascertain the true state of affairs, before disinvesting them of all important documents appertaining to the case (legal jargon, PP found, was catching).

At last the great day for setting out arrived. Having loaded the luggage, the children squashed into the back of the car. Petunia and Furball were perched in the front alongside the world's worse driver, Ivy ffrench-Fawcett.

Ivy was in high good humour. Just wanted to be there when old PP came face to face with the heap of stone which would be all that remained of the old place. 'What a hoot it will be!' she laa-de-daa'd to herself, as she threw the car around corners, flinging everyone up and down and out of their seats. Even Furball began to keep his eyes closed after a few miles. It was worse than trying to ride the wall of death.

After what seemed like days, even though it had only been half an hour or so, Ivy suddenly side-swiped into a small sleepy village, skidding gravel everywhere, and screeched to a halt outside a small building. A tiny metal sign, squealing in the wind above the door, announced in faded lettering that this was the premises of 'Sniv... ...ivell º ...ouch Ltd.' PP (who no longer wore her glasses as she felt they damaged her glamour image) ordered Vicky out to see if this was indeed the offices of Snivell, Snivell & Crouch. Then out she stormed, closely shadowed by Ivy, and in she strode without a knock. Inside, a young woman was busily painting her nails fire-engine red.

'I'm here to see Mr. Snivell,' snapped PP.

'Senior or Junior,' simpered the nail-painter, blowing on them to harden the polish.

'Senior,' said PP who always believed in starting at the top.

'Mr Snivell Senior is out on business.'

'Then I'll see Snivell Junior,' declared the witch, ready for war, her face set for battle.

'He's away,' said the bimbo. 'It's the Long Vac, or the Bank Holiday, whichever comes first ... twitter ... twitter ...!'

'What about Crouch?' snapped PP. 'Out with gout?'

Replacing the polish in her desk, the bimbo smiled charmingly and asked to whom she had the pleasure of speaking.

'Petunia Pennefeather and companion,' put in Ivy helpfully.

A strange look came over the face behind the desk as she faltered, 'The Castle Bashford heiress...'

Petunia growled that she didn't have all day to chat to office staff. She just wanted the details of her inheritance and have them she would — even if it meant staying here all day long. But try as she might, the bimbo pussyfooted about with lots of 'I can't say...' and 'I'm not allowed to give out that information...' and 'Perhaps you could come back tomorrow ... or the day after ...' In the end they left, PP having ordered Mr Snivell to contact them soonest.

'If I should wish to sell the property, I'll need the deeds,' finished PP.

'Need what?' said the bimbo, who hadn't been listening.

'Need to discuss the handing over of the deeds,' said Vicky, ushering the witch away.

PP groaned as she whipped out her cold tea-bags and settled back into her seat. 'I don't think she heard me saying I would sell the property,' she grumbled. 'You shouldn't have interrupted.'

'Never sell a pig in a poke,' said Vicky.

'Frustrating,' summed up Ivy as they bounced along. 'But there was nothing else you could have done. At least you are spared the expense of a meeting. The way these solicitors chalk up "attendance" fees. . .!'

They drove on at a furious pace until they came to Ballyonder. Ivy halted so abruptly that Furball almost went through the front window, and poking her floppy hat out of the window she enquired of a yokel who was propping up a wall, 'Are we on the right road for Bashford Castle?'

'Aye,' mumbled the yokel, dazed by the sight of a stuffed bird on a hat. 'Keeping going on up the boreen, past the white stones painted yellow, through the "No Entry" gate, and keep right at the "No Right Turn" sign.'

The children giggled helplessly. 'Clear as mud,' whispered Jassy.

'Ta,' chortled Ivy, delighted that it was only a matter

of time before they caught sight of PP's pile of rubble. 'No doubt you're wondering,' she went on to no one in particular, 'how I find my way so easily? We ffrench-Fawcetts have navigational skills which date back to the dawn of civilisation. Hunting, and all that. . .'

She mounted the ditch to avoid a petrified cyclist who was blessing himself in fright. Furball closed his eyes and decided to sleep; he had a couple of lives to spare.

Jassy wriggled about uncomfortably, wedged in behind Joey and his fishing-rod. The girls were trying not to let it get tangled in PP's elaborate earrings, which might have caused another riot.

'This must be it,' quacked Ivy, as they neared an old crumbling building with enormous nettles poking out everywhere. 'Well, it *is* rustic. And I dare say the view from the top is charming. Pet-oonia, dear! I can see the newspaper headlines — *Prices slump as castle stocks hit the ground.*'

'Snooks,' sniffed PP, staring out.

A bawneen cap appeared over the wall, followed by a voice enquiring, 'What would ye be wanting?'

'Is this Bashford Castle?' croaked PP.

' 'Tis surely,' said the man. ' 'Tis all the land of Castle Bashford in these parts.'

Everyone, except Ivy, felt really disappointed.

'It would seem,' grumbled Petunia, as everyone started at the heap of weathered stones. 'It would seem we've arrived a tad on the late side.'

'A tad?' skitted Ivy. 'More like nine hundred and ninety-nine years. Hee, hee!'

'Would ye be tourists or a class of visitor?' asked the man, peering at the odd collection of faces which gaped at him through the misted car windows.

'Actually,' twittered Ivy, pointing at PP. 'Actually she's the heiress to this heap of rubble.' She turned away her head, unsuccessfully trying to keep a straight face.

'Well, is that a possible fact?' said the man, leaning on the outside of the door. 'Scut Fagin's the name and I'm pleased to meet you.'

'No relation, I trust?' snapped the witch. 'Can't say I return the compliment.'

The man roared with laughter. 'A Pennefeather for sure!'

'I'm absolutely ravenous,' interrupted Ivy. 'Is there anywhere we might get a bite to eat, Mr. Err...?'

'Scut, to your good self, Mam. Well there's plenty of pubs but you're sure to be welcome above in the big place.'

'Big place?' echoed everyone.

'Sure amn't I after telling you? It's all Castle Bashford round here. That,' pointing, 'is the road up to the castle. The finest castle in Ireland!'

'You mean...' faltered the crestfallen Ivy. 'You mean the castle is still standing?'

'In the finest working order,' said Scut.

The children craned their necks out of the fogged-up windows as they rounded a corner and there it was...! A great castle, built of beautifully cut stone, standing in magnificent grounds, with parapets, ramparts, mullioned windows, the lot! A large heraldic banner fluttered over the battlements. Everyone was stunned into complete silence.

'Wow!' thought Furball.

5

A Hornets' Nest

Ivy was the first to recover. She rammed the gearstick, causing the car to cough alarmingly. Then they shot forwards at 100 miles an hour.

'How well it looks . . . considering it has been uninhabited for years,' remarked PP as the castle came into sharper focus.

'Uninhabited? Pet-oonia, dear,' simpered Ivy as she rounded the side of the castle and skidded to a stop, almost pranging the wing of a big gold-coloured Volvo which was parked in a long line of expensive-looking cars. 'These cars would suggest that the castle is far from being uninhabited. . .'

They all fell out of the car in great excitement, the girls stiff with pins and needles, Joey moaning that his rod was bent beyond repair. Petunia stalked up the stone steps, her back as straight as a ramrod (a sure sign of displeasure). The rest pushed after her through the great doorway, dying to see what would happen next.

They found themselves in an enormous hall with deep carpets and magnificent antique furniture. Soft tinkling music was playing and there were huge flower arrangements everywhere. The children marvelled at the knight's suit of armour pinned to the wall. Ivy studied the oriental pots and vases with deep interest; why hadn't she thought of a Salon Chinoise. . .?

Just as Petunia was about to push the brass bell on the reception desk a group of ladies came jogging down the great staircase chanting, 'A moment on the lips, a lifetime on the hips'. PP gaped as they jogged past her, out through the door and down the steps.

She slammed the bell hard.

A portly gentleman surfaced behind the desk. 'You rang, Moddom?'

'Correct,' glared PP. 'I rang ... and what I...'

'Does Moddom have a reservation?' he asked in a cool polished voice.

'What...?' screeched PP, grabbing the poor man by his neat silk tie. 'What I want to know is what exactly you lot are doing in *my* castle?'

'*Your* castle. A likely story! This is an hotel, Moddom, I'm Philpot. I and my staff have been trained with honours at the National College of Catering and the Ballyhoo School of Cookery. The rich and famous of the world come here for peace and quiet.'

'Not from now on,' thought Furball, as a scream rose from PP.

'Listen, Potshot. I don't care who you are. I'm the owner and I can prove it. Now take yourself and this potty lot out of here immediately — if not sooner!'

'Out! Out! Out!' she barked at the dumbstruck guests of Bashford Castle, who had just been about to order themselves afternoon tea (the Thursday Special with clotted cream and upside-down raspberry turnovers, served in the Bogoak Lounge or the Granuaile Conservatory from 4.30 to 5.30 pm).

To cries of 'She must be mad,' 'Send for the Fire Brigade,' 'Send for the ambulance,' 'Send for Snivell, Snivell & Crouch,' Petunia rushed into the gardens to gather her reeling wits. It need hardly be said that she was in a furious rage. No wonder Snivell, Snivell & Crouch had been so evasive. No wonder they had

been collectively unavailable. They hadn't made the faintest attempt to look for her — Petunia Pennefeather, the rightful owner of all this. They had seen an opportunity and grabbed it. While she was living in penury amid straitened circumstances, they had been living on the fat of the land. They had found the pot of gold at the end of the rainbow!

As she paced to and fro between the boxwood edging, her anger gradually subsided. It is not generally known but once the furious temper of the Pennefeathers subsides they become quite (well, almost quite) reasonable. Shuddering to think that she had ever written off the castle as a pile of rubbish, had been the point of refusing to go and see it, and had even thought of selling it off to avoid taxes, PP gradually succumbed to the charm of her surroundings. The scent of the boxwood mingled with that of the roses, the birds were singing symphonies, and there was the distant sound of fountains playing. The shadow of the battlements falling across the velvet-smooth lawns aroused in her feelings she had long thought dead.

'Oh, to own such a noble pile! To see the Pennefeather coat of arms (a cat rampant, holding in his dexter paw a dagger piercing a card) floating from the top-most tower! To be the lady of the manor!' Oh yes; PP remembered the good old days with a tear in her eye. For years she had suffered the indignity of penury in a small cottage, patronised by Ivy and ridiculed by the do-gooders. If only...

The accidental stubbing of her toe against an antique urn brought her to her senses. It wasn't a dream! She, Petunia Pennefeather, was the owner of the most magnificent castle in Ireland. Now that wealth and position had been restored she'd show everyone that, having seen the two sides of life, the Pennefeather breeding and class would enable her to take on the burden of being a Leader of Society ... yak ... yak...

She was still muttering to herself when she arrived back in the Great Hall. Snivell Senior was no longer 'out'. The Number One Card (Non Availability) had failed. He had come in from the cold and was telling everyone to 'remain calm and await further developments'.

'Everything is under control — abso...lutely no problem!' he gushed.

PP attacked him from behind and buttonholed him into a chair, hissing, 'You had better explain yourself before I have you struck off the Register of Solicitors in Ireland and make you eat your parchment for dessert.'

Snivell Senior decided to play Card Number Two (Suck-up to and/or Patronise the Customer).

'My dear young lady,' he smiled, showing a set of teeth of which a shark would not have been ashamed. 'This has all been a most *unfortunate* misunderstanding ... crave indulgence ... best intentions ... castle in danger of becoming a ruin ...blot on the landscape ... threat to the environment ... target for Greenpeace ... a constant worry to the firm ... everything taken care of ... no need to worry your pretty little head...'

For once, Card Number Two fell flat on its face. PP fixed Snivell Senior with a stony stare.

'Now you listen to me,' she stormed. 'I want everything here by 9 am. On the dot. Tomorrow morning. Deeds. Accounts. Tax payments. Profit projections. Cash in hand. Cash at the bank. Are you clear?'

Snivell Senior ran a hot sticky finger inside his shirt collar which seemed to be tightening by the minute.

'But I thought you were thinking of selling?'

'What on earth gave you that ridiculous idea!'

'But you said ... in the office...'

'He must have been listening at the keyhole,' thought Vicky.

'Your secretary must be hard of hearing. If she spent less time polishing her nails and more time clearing out her ears, she might get her messages straight. Now, get cracking.'

'If you would care to make an appointment,' suggested Snivell Senior, fighting a rearguard action. 'My secretary will phone you and let you know when I'm available.'

'Tomorrow. HERE. Not there. 9 sharp! In the Alcock and Brown Study.'

So saying, PP swept from the Great Hall. The guests who were still around were all rooted to the spot. This was no ordinary hotel, and that was certain!

'What's all this about "Out! Out! Out!"?' asked one.

'We're not going anywhere!' said a tanned man dressed in oilskins, with fishing flies sticking out of his hat. 'It's taken us years to hire that wily old Scut Fagin to show us exactly where the Deep Pool is up river and nothing and nobody is going to interfere with our fishing holiday for the next two weeks.'

'I have a feeling there is going to be trouble,' said Vicky to Jassy.

'Trouble?' thought Furball. 'That's putting it mildly.'

When Petunia reswept her way down into the Great Hall a short time later it was empty except for Philpot. He eyed her uneasily.

Luckily, just at that moment, a group of tourists, armed to the teeth with maps and historical documents and cameras dangling everywhere, decanted themselves from a bus.

Mistaking PP for a cleaner (she being dressed in black and carrying a broom) they ordered her to remove the mud from the bus.

'It's so muddy over here!' they whined. 'And the highways are impossible ... and everyone drives on the wrong side of the road ... and the exchange rate is so poor for dollars ...whinge, whinge ... and nobody seems to know where Grand Pappy's buried ... whinge, whinge.' They stopped to gather breath for more complaining.

'Is that so?' said PP, dangerously polite. 'And WHO...' she continued, 'who asked you to come in the first place, might I ask?'

The tourists, who had become used to complaining nonstop, suddenly found themselves stumped. Nobody had ever had the nerve to ask them such a question before.

Grinning all round his fat cigar, the biggest of the party, Marty Capone, said, 'Honey, I just love your Irish sense of humour!'

'Yeah, really quaint,' agreed the rest of the party. 'I guess this is the sort of humour our great ancestors enjoyed.'

They trundled upstairs, taking even more photographs, and practising their 'Begorras' and 'Top of the morning to you', which, they had been assured, would see them safely through any language difficulties.

Joey giggled, but Vicky sent a pained expression heavenwards.

Who knows what might have happened next had not a dapper gentleman, bursting with good humour, apeared in the Hall.

'Ah, Mr Hanratty,' said the highly relieved Philpot. 'This is . . . this is. . .' He indicated PP.

'I know. Allow me to introduce myself, Ms Pennefeather. I'm Hanratty the Manager. Allow me to offer you tea in my sitting-room.' Leading the way, with PP, Ivy and the children in tow, he continued. 'Snivell, Snivell & Crouch have explained to me that you know nothing about the castle. Allow me to explain. . .'

PP opened her mouth to make a crushing rejoinder, but Hanratty continued without pausing for breath, 'When your Greatuncle died so unexpectedly. . .'

'. . . at the age of 92?' thought Furball.

'. . . and no family appeared, it fell to *someone* to decide what should be done.'

'I missed the death notice,' muttered PP through clenched teeth, which was hardly surprising as she only took the paper every second day.

'Always knew that was false economy,' thought Furball.

'We advertised for you *everywhere. The Beekeepers' Gazette, The Antiques Yearbook, The Aged & Indigent Vegetarians' Handbook, The Cat-lovers' Annual Manual, The DIY Guide to Cottage Homes, The Homedressmaker's Magazine.* . .'

'What a collection!' thought Furball. '*Stars of the Silver Screen* would have got her in one.'

'Did the old man die penniless?' asked Ivy with great interest.

'Oh, far from it!' said the jolly Hanratty. 'But the upkeep of a castle of this size — maintenance, gardens, heating costs, staff, stables, riparian rights — are absolutely *enormous.* My father-in-law, senior partner in the old-established firm of Snivell, Snivell & Crouch, came up with the brainwave of turning the castle — literally a white elephant at that stage — into a luxury hotel where people who long for good old-fashioned Irish hospitality can come and enjoy peace and good food.

'It was all done from the *purest* of motives — purely for the benefit of the inheritors or inheritor when they/ he/she surfaced. I can't tell you what Mr Snivell Senior had been through in the last ten years. Every year added five more to his life. Grey hairs. A stoop. Palsy — you've noticed how he shakes?'

'I think that was PP, not palsy,' thought Furball.

'Some brainwave!' gritted PP, suddenly strangely unable to kick a man who was lying at her feet, four paws up. She might have been able to manage it had she seen Snivell Senior, who was at that very moment denuding the safe of all the loose cash on the premises.

'I'm sure you'll be *most* impressed when you've had time to take it all in,' said Mr Hanratty, sensing that the moment of physical danger had passed him by. 'Now, perhaps you'd like to freshen up before dinner ... I've arranged rooms for you and your party...'

He winked at the children, who were enjoying the situation enormously.

'And, of course, there is a courtesy BMW at your disposal at all times.'

The girls had a room en suite. So had the boys. Ivy declared she was going to sink into her sunken bath, and PP, conscious that she was being taken for a ride, fumed in the Presidential Suite.

The phone rang at seven — to inform them that the dinner-gong was gonging downstairs and they might like to make their way dinnerwards. Just as Ivy was about to knock on PP's door, out swanned the witch in a black and green (rather well creased) taffeta skirt.

Her straggly hair had been strangled into a tortoise-shell comb, making her seem unnaturally presentable.

'Cripey,' scoffed Joey. 'If it ain't Ivana Frump!'

Everyone fell about the place laughing. They often wondered just how the witch always managed to find an outfit for every occasion from an old carpet-bag and a battered hat-box.

'Make yourself presentable,' she ordered Joey, who was complaining loudly to the girls that he didn't like wearing a sissy jacket and pointed yuppie shoes.

Down in the Great Hall, people were appearing from every corner. All were dressed for pre-dinner drinks with vast amounts of jewellery and strings of pearls. A large party of somberly suited businessmen, no doubt suffering from 'executive stress', appeared from an ante-room where they had apparently been having an 'off the cuff' briefing session, declaring to all that 'Bank interest rates must rise'.

As the witch's party arrived at the turn of the stairs leading down to the Great Hall, Mr Hanratty clapped his hands for silence and announced:

'May I present the owner of Bashford Castle and her party.'

Everyone gathered in the lounge paused to observe the pretty tableau, and then resumed their conversations, surreptitiously casting glances from time to time at the party of six, who were by now ensconced by the grand piano.

The children, in turn, stared at the guests, whispering to each other, 'They look terribly well off and everything.'

'Suppose PP starts one of her "evils-of-money" lectures,' worried Tansy.

A circle of burly bodyguards appeared, checking out the area before a small, foreign-looking man, wearing flowing Arab robes and head-dress, appeared.

He nodded a greeting to the guests, who all bowed saying, 'Good evening, Sheik Ahab Crashoggi.'

'That's all we need!' muttered PP. 'Bad enough to have one's house full of dreadful tourists! But to have it full of foreigners who've stolen the bed linen and the tablecloths — well, that really is the limit!'

'Shssh,' whispered Vicky. 'You'll start an International Incident.'

A piper dressed in full regalia ('We'll have him in the Pennefeather tartan shortly,' said PP grandly) and carrying a huge set of pipes played them into dinner in the impressive Corrib Country dining-room. This, explained PP, was an old Irish custom when kin occupied the castle. Ivy, who rather fancied this way of life, enquired if the piper was available for dinner-parties and the odd musical evening.

'Hands off!' glared PP as they tucked into deliciously cooked food, served by a venerable old retainer who kept asking 'If there was anything else your Ladyship would be requiring?'

Just before the end of the meal, PP rose like a rook, glided across the room and disappeared.

'She's overcome with all this splendour.' Ivy, whose nose was feeling decidedly out of joint, grasped at this small straw of consolation as she demolished a double second helping of ice-cream which she polished off at a rate of knots. ('It's not nearly as fattening if you eat it quickly,' she explained.)

Returning to PP, she went on, 'Must be difficult. The sudden elevation from penury to plenty. From ruin to riches. From misery to the magnificence of

Bashford. It has all been too much for her. You have to be born to it ... like us ffrench-Fawcetts.'

The truth was that PP had suddenly thought about the safe and was even now staring at a load of emptiness. 'Just wait till I get my hands on that Snivell,' she fumed.

Later that night as Victoria and Tansy climbed into their great big four-poster bed they wondered aloud, 'Wonder where PP got to? Do we know? Do we care?' They fell asleep.

An hour later PP was banging on their door, yelling. 'It's *your* job to think of a way to empty the castle of these mealy-bugs of tourists ... or else...'

But her voice was drowned out by the loud Zzz...Zzz...Zzz... coming from behind the bedroom door.

Somewhere in their sub-conscious something must have registered, because at 6 am precisely Vicky woke with a start, shook Tansy and hissed, 'Get the boys ... we'd better get busy...'

6

PP Has a Brainwave

Next morning when everyone came down to breakfast they were dazzled by big gaudy signs everywhere...

The Americans were busy taking photographs — delighted by 'real cute Irish signs'. The management was aghast. Philpot looked like he was having a heart attack on the spot and the jolly Hanratty could hardly raise a smile.

PP was unavailable. She spent all day in her suite. Snivell Senior had not materialised at 9 am; he had sent over an ancient clerk who left at reception a black plastic sack full of legal documents, account books, bank statements, thick files of correspondence from ill-minded busy-bodies threatening legal action over rights of way and river pollution, claims from tourists alleging food poisoning, overbooking, and near fatal accidents sustained while balancing on the battlements.

And bills, bills, bills. . . It seemed that Snivell, Snivell & Crouch, while a dab hand at raking in the cash, had drawn the line at disgorging any of it. The whole thing gave her such a headache that she retired to bed. The final straw had been an estimate for essential repairs to the roof . . . copper . . . concrete . . . lead . . . bricks . . . time and materials . . . £9999.99! With a footnote drawing attention of client to the imminent collapse of said roof unless. . .

Furball was deputed to march up and down outside the Presidential Suite, carrying a banner with DO NOT DISTURB written on it.

'Here I am,' thought PP to herself, having thrown everything back into the plastic sack. 'A poor lone woman, defenceless against the Snivells of the world. And down there, eating their heads off, are the brains of the world banking system. People who can read a Balance-Sheet upside down. Men who know a Debit from a Credit. If only I could get one of them to. . .' She sat bolt upright. 'Why shouldn't I nab one of them? I'd have no further financial worries. Why that £9999.99 would be chicken-feed to any of them . . . probably get more in pocket-money. *He* could go on living here and *I'd* get a bit of peace and quiet. I deserve it. Onward, Petunia! Think of our motto. . .'

Petunia swanned down for dinner, much to everyone's surprise, dressed in pale green *peau-de-soie* with a yellow carnation stuck behind her ear. In the Bogoak Lounge, just as she was about to sidle past a thick-set American tourist, her lace handkerchief fluttered to the ground. He picked it up and in they went, arm-in-arm, to dinner.

''I don't believe it,' said Vicky at the other end of the table.

'Believe what?' asked Joey who was, as usual, rather slow on the uptake.

'That's Hiram H Hinkelheimer IV?' said Ivy, her eyes round as saucers; she had been checking up on the guest list. 'He's worth MILLIONS!'

'BILLIONS!' corrected Vicky.

'Do you think they...?' asked Tansy.

'But he's ancient,' contributed Jassy. 'Why he must be a hundred and two,' meaning at least thirty-five.

'Well it takes one autumn chicken to know another,' said Vicky darkly.

The next morning at breakfast in PP's Presidential Suite, she was all smiles.

'Oh, what a wonderful morning,' she carolled as she threw open the casement window.

'We thought up some new ideas,' said Vicky. 'What do you think of...'

Mysterious lysteria – you'll find it here.

'Or,' put in Jassy, who had been awake half the night churning out brainstorms...

We have the steak you love to eat,
For Angel Dust is hard to beat

It took PP a little while to come back to earth. She stared at the signs.

'Oh, Vicky dear,' she said in an unusually pleasant voice. 'What are all those tatty signs doing down in the Great Hall? Anyone reading them would almost think we wanted our honoured guests to leave'

As everyone stared blankly, she continued, 'Do make sure they're all removed before anyone comes down for breakfast. So inhospitable. Where's our famous Irish welcome?' She poured herself a cup of coffee from a George IV coffee-pot, with baluster body chased with two scroll-leaf cartouches engraved with crest below vertical flutes (1823), stirred in a gentle Hester Bates teaspoon of sugar, and just a tweeny bit of cream from an Irish helmet cream-jug with lion mask and paw feet, chased with flowers (George Moore of Limerick).

Having taken a leaf or two from Ivy's Grand Tour, she had boned up on the inventory and was now in a position to dazzle everyone with chunks from auctioneers' catalogues.

Furball, who had pricked up his ears at the sound of the cream-jug being lifted, said to himself, 'Sickening for something. Definitely a case of the old delirious tremolos.'

'For some odd reason,' went on PP, her cup of coffee held between hands propped on two skinny elbows, which rested, contrary to polite usage, on the table. 'I've been thinking a lot lately about gems. I had always thought that diamonds were a girl's best friend, but

now I'm not so sure. Emeralds — their green fire brings
out something in me — as Hiram whispered to me
last night. Or rubies — there's something in that intense
red heart that seems to echo the blaze I appear to kindle
in others — as Hiram told me yesterday afternoon in
the conservatory. Or sapphires — are their cold icy
depths a reflection of that perfection that makes me
seem so unattainable. . .?'

The children listened with eyes growing rounder by
the minute. Being in love obviously turned tough old
hearts into mush, not to mention addling the brain.

'Definitely round the bend,' thought Furball. 'I'd
better get in some fast snoozing. There's going to be
a rude awakening, any hour now.'

Before he drifted off the sleep he heard PP saying
confidentally to Vicky, 'It's only a question of time
before he offers.'

'Offers what?' asked Joey.

'Be quiet,' hissed Vicky. 'That's the old-fashioned
way of saying he's going to propose marriage.'

'About the wedding dress?' continued PP. 'Whether
white or not?' (She secretly fancied something with
millions of sequins but regretfully ruled it out.) 'Of
course nothing looks so ridiculous as someone of, say,
over thirty-five wearing white. But for anyone under
thirty, I think it has to be the choice. So fresh. . .'

'Aged one hundred and two or not,' said Vicky, when
the children gathered for a post-mortem. 'She's hooked.'

'Will she be the fourth Mrs Hiram H Hinkelheimer?'
asked Joey, who hadn't quite got the hang of American
dynasties.

'No, idiot, Mrs Hiram H Hinkelheimer IV!'

'She told me,' said Tansy, 'that it is every girl's duty to

accept a man with money.'

'Probably thinking of the roof,' put in Joey.

'And the dry-rot and the death-watch beetle.'

'You could be right,' said Vicky slowly. 'She spent all day yesterday looking at the accounts . . . and then came out and nabbed him.'

'Maybe *he* thinks *she* has money,' said Jassy darkly. This was so funny that they fell about laughing.

'Anyway,' said Vicky briskly. 'Why worry? We've nothing to lose. If Hiram H Hinkelheimer comes up with a few million, why should we complain? And if he doesn't, we've still got the castle. At least as long as Hiram H is around, Operation Tourists-Out can be suspended. Let's enjoy ourselves!'

So while PP and Hiram H held hands and looked deep into each other's eyes, Joey and Jassy fished tirelessly, and the girls played tennis, went pony trekking on the castle's Connemara ponies, and made full use of the sauna, the jacuzzi and beauty parlour.

Ivy, who had gone home for a few days, returned to find the Great Romance in full swing, thereby causing further nose disjointing. PP was all honied sympathy. 'No wonder she's back. Once she had seen the splendours of Bashford, evidently couldn't stand that tawdry Hatter's Hall, with all its fake antiques. . .'

Ivy consoled herself with lavish meals and PP's BMW. At first it was just the 'odd little runabout' – to keep the tyres from perishing. But as she rather fancied herself as a Grand Prix driver, she soon spent most of her time careering about the lanes. The natives were scared witless; at the sight of her approaching they legged it into the nearest ditch, or if frozen into immobility, closed their eyes and said their prayers.

7
Bewitched, Bothered and Bewildered...

PP was in irritable humour. After a splendid dinner she had suggested a walk by the lake. Surely, with a full moon overhead and the strains of *Mick McGinty's Goat* floating after them across the lawns, the moment of proposal must be nigh. But Hiram H had been acting rather strangely these last few days and instead of jumping at the idea of a walk in the moonlight he pleaded a headache and went off to bed, with a glass of hot milk and a hot-water bottle.

Alone in the Presidential Suite, PP pondered upon her next move. Now (as you know) PP was not the kind of witch who can sit still and wait for things to happen. No! If the mountain wouldn't come to Petunia, then Petunia would go to the mountain.

She decided to knock upon his door and invite him down for a nightcap. Surely he would be so touched by her solicitude that he could hardly refuse. Throwing on her cape she hurried out of the Suite and along the corridor. She wasn't quite sure of the number of Hiram's room but that was no problem; she would knock on every door.

Just as she was about to knock on the first door, she heard the voice of jolly Hanratty floating around a corner. Petunia froze. He was the last person she wanted to meet. Without knocking, she dodged into the nearest room and rested against the door, waiting for her chance to escape. Across the room she saw an open window.

'That will do nicely,' she muttered to herself.

Just as she took a step towards it a voice called, 'Is that you, Mildew honey?'

The muffled voice seemed to be coming from the bed in the centre of the darkened room. PP recognised it in a flash.

It was the voice of Hiram H Hinkelheimer IV, her laggard suitor!

'Speak to me, Mildew. Don't you recognise me? Hiram, your dear husband,' wailed the voice from the bed.

PP was in a quandary. She couldn't retreat back through the door, not with that wretched Hanratty lurking about; the thought of his face, were he to see her emerging from the bedroom of Hiram H Hinkelheimer, rooted her to the spot. Nor could she make for the window; Hiram would undoubtedly suspect a burglar and raise the alarm. Her blood ran cold at the thought of the jolly Hanratty and the entire guest list rushing to the rescue.

Quick as a flash she answered in a thin little voice, 'Ye. . .ss, Hiram dear . . . It is I, Mildew.'

'Oh, Mildew, I always knew you'd come back to me. I need your help. My stocks and shares. . .'

'Ha . . . Snooks,' muttered PP.

'Smokes?' said Hiram, thinking Mildew was referring to his smoking. 'Consider it done. Not another cigar shall sit on my lips, Mildew . . . now, about the stock market. I've had a lot of bad breaks lately. . .'

Petunia froze in her tracks, then relaxed. After all, what's a million among billions! It pleased her in a way to find that dear Hiram thought only of money, even when he was half asleep. Without the shadow of a doubt – ideal husband material.

'But I've had one great stroke of luck lately, Mildew. I've met this . . . fantastically . . . rich woman. Owns a castle. Land. Fisheries. And she's eating out of my hand. What should I do, Mildew?' His voice rose to a wail. 'I want to be true to your memory. . .'

'So you're thinking of marrying this rich woman?' PP's voice had a dangerous edge to it.

'It doesn't mean a thing, Mildew honey. But it's a shame to think of all that money going to waste. With a stack like that I could get right back on top. I must do something, Mildew, I'm practically penniless. Mildew honey, you do understand. . .'

'Understand?' screamed PP, seizing Hiram's silver-plated walking-stick – the one with the duck's head – and belabouring him with it. 'Take that . . . and that . . .' thrashing wildly at the body in the bed.

'Oh Mildew honey, don't take on so,' said the distraught Hiram. 'You know it means nothing. All I want is her money.'

'And take that too!' PP's final blow, which almost decapitated Hiram, shattered the walking-stick. It broke into several pieces, leaving PP with the duck's head.

As sounds escalated in the corridor – the officious Hanratty, hearing Hiram's screams, must have alerted the entire castle – PP rushed to the window. Hiram's voice pursued her.

'But about my stocks? Should I sell by the new moon or wait for a bull market? Give me some advice, Mildew. If I don't marry this woman, I need one quick killing to restore the Hiram H Hinkelheimer fortunes.'

PP, dashing up on to the window-ledge, muttered, 'Keep your feet dry and wear wellies,' before jumping out into the night.

On hearing the muffled message, Hiram H sat bolt upright with excitement. "Bellies. Pork bellies, she said. Pork bellies. Why didn't I think of that? Hot dog!'

The last the witch heard as she landed in the bushes with a heavy thump was dear old Hiram's voice drifting out through the window shouting, 'Wall Street. Hello, Wall Street. I wanna buy one million shares in Pork Bellies. . .'

'I hope he loses every last cent,' she thought savagely, raging through the undergrowth. She shinned across the grass and tried the front door. It was locked.

'Hanratty's too good at the security business,' she growled unreasonably. However, in no time at all, she had managed to unpick the lock, using a large old earring she just happened to have in her pocket. She sneaked towards the kitchen to pour herself a glass of hooch.

'One spirit to another!' she chuckled as she raised her glass.

As PP emerged into the Great Hall, preparatory to

going upstairs, it seemed that the entire staff and guest list were assembled there.

'A terrible event has just happened,' explained Hanratty. 'Poor Mr Hinkelheimer has been attacked. In his bed.'

'Any injuries? Nothing trivial, I hope.'

'We've just sent for the doctor. And the police.'

'Any clues?' PP fingered the duck's head in her pocket, thinking to herself that if the entire staff and every guest in the castle had been rushing around the room this was highly unlikely.

'Well, I must get off to bed. Mustn't miss my beauty sleep,' she yawned. It occurred to her that everyone was looking at her strangely. Then she suddenly recollected that Hiram had, after all, been half of the great romantic team. Shedding a little tear, she said, 'Poor Hiram. I'll send him flowers in the morning.'

At the top of the stairs she turned and said, 'Let this be a lesson to you all. No good comes of going to bed early with hot milk and hot-water bottles.'

8

A Red-Letter Day

Early next morning the old PP came to life. She called a meeting in the Grace O'Malley study (lined with 'picturesque views over the lovely Achill Island to the ruins of an ancient O'Malley stronghold, now a ruin').

The children cancelled appointments and assembled sullenly.

'Now, get this straight,' said PP, leaping to the attack. 'It's about time you lot did a little work around here. I'm slaving my fingers to the bone over hot balance-sheets and what are you doing?' Adopting a mincing tone she went on, 'Tennis, fishing, shooting and hunting, riding, hair appointments ... It's all got to stop.'

'But...' began Vicky.

'Silence!' thundered the witch. 'If I've asked you once, I've asked you a hundred times to ... get rid of those dratted tourists. Yet every morning when I come down they're still there, wearing out the carpets, polluting the air. And every evening when I come down to dinner in my ancestral hall, they're still there ... acting as if they owned the place.'

'But we did try,' squeaked Tansy.

'Apple-pie beds,' contributed Joey. This involved folding the top sheet back half way, causing whoever got into bed to whack their knees off their chin.

'Mixing up all the shoes left out for polishing,' added Jassy.

'Organising a whispering campaign to tell them the

drains had been condemned by Queen Victoria,' ended Vicky.

'Huh... Useless. Worse than useless. All you pesky brats have done is to make Bashford Castle more attractive. Listen to this,' and she read aloud from a postcard which had been entrusted to the Bashford Castle post-office for safe transmission to the USA and/ or the ends of the earth:

Honey! Having the MOST exciting time. A thrill a minute! Something new every day! So Irish! Drop everything and join us.'

As the children stood, downcast, the witch shrilled, 'It's got to stop before we're completely taken over. I want — this time tomorrow — from each of you — three good ideas for getting rid of these crawling nuisances. And they'd better be good — and effective — or else...'

'That's hardly fair,' defended Vicky. 'We did try — earlier. Then you told us to stop...'

'Silence!' roared the witch. 'In the meanwhile, I want that thing on the battlements changed. That flag.'

They all looked up to the tower on which it fluttered in the breeze — two boars entwined with snakes, fessways, behind a sinister hand with club. Motto: Gardez bien (hold fast).

'Joey,' fixing him with a gimlet eye. 'Shin up there, take down that wretched Snivell emblem — the confounded cheek of that outfit — and put up the ancestral Pennefeather flag.'

'Where will I get it?' stuttered Joey who had no great head for heights.

'Make one, you dumb-wit. Get these layabouts to help you. The Pennefeather arms are a cat rampant, holding in his dexter paw a dagger piercing a card, triple-towered castle in background, en or. Motto: Touch not the cat.'

Furball, who had been asleep on the window-sill, woke up just in time to hear the ancient motto trotted out. 'Splendid! So I do have a place in the scheme of things,' he murmured to himself before he drowsed off again, just failing to hear her add, '... without a glove...'

'How unfair ... to poor Furball,' said Vicky.

'And another thing,' barked the witch, clearly in a getting-things-done frame of mind. 'From now on the castle will be known as *Bats*ford Castle, not *Bash*ford. Batsford.'

'Pet-oonia, dear, do you think that is wise?' queried Ivy, who had just appeared clutching a letter marked 'Special Delivery'. 'Bashford is an ancient historic name, marked on all the ordnance survey maps. You just can't change it like that.'

'And why not?' roared PP. 'Most certainly a corruption of an ancient Irish name in the first place. Bashford ... Huh! They meant Batsford, of course.'

'Bats?' Ivy's hair stood on end. 'Nasty things. Get in your hair.'

'Stuff and nonsense. Bats are perfectly splendid creatures. Keep down insects. Fertilise fruits. Propagate seed. Do untold good. But what would you know about it? Bet you couldn't tell a Pipistrelle from a Lesser Horseshoe or a Natterer's from a Large Mouse-eared.'

'I only...' quavered Ivy, recoiling before the onslaught and handing over the letter, '... came to bring this in to you. It's urgent.'

PP glared at her and took the letter.

'More pestilent tourists, I'll be bound,' she nattered

as she opened it. Out popped a letterheading with the sinister trio of names: SNIVELL, SNIVELL & CROUCH.

Vicky, looking over her shoulders could just about read the contents. It was headed:

ESTATE OF THE LATE LORD FRUZEY-BROWNE, BT

Dear Madam:
We are writing to advise you that our client, Angeline (Bibi), widow of the late Fruzey Few-Browne, Bt, Deceased, is claiming a share of the above estate.

In our opinion she is entitled to a two-third share of the estate.

We remain,
Your humble servants,
SNIVELL, SNIVELL & CROUCH.

'The cheek of them,' roared PP. 'Kept me out of my inheritance for years. Now they want to take it off me altogether.'

'If I may put in a word,' said Ivy helpfully. 'I happen to know about these things.'

PP glared but as no sound actually passed her lips, Ivy went on, 'The widow is, as you know, under the Succession Act of 1969, Section III, sub-section 4, clause 4z, entitled to a two-third share of the spouse's estate, if there was no will. . .'

'But there was a will,' croaked PP. 'That idiot of a young Snivell read it to me himself.'

'But was it legal?' Ivy was so sympathetic. 'Your uncle *probably* intended to leave you his estate. But maybe he didn't sign the will. Maybe it wasn't witnessed. People at death's door often do the most stupid things.'

'I'll fight it to the death,' shouted PP.

'. . . but even if the will is perfectly all right, it still doesn't alter the fact that, by law, your uncle had to leave a one-third share to his widow.'

As PP seemed still in a state of shock, Ivy went on, 'Try and look for the silver lining, in this case the will. After all, if it *was* a legal will, you still get to keep two-thirds of the estate. It's a lot better than one-third, isn't it?'

'What will they do?' whispered Tansy to Vicky. 'Split the castle three ways.'

'She'll have to sell it,' whispered Vicky back. 'And make a cash settlement.'

"I'll bet old Snivell himself buys it back — for a song,' ventured Joey.

Much the same sequence of thought must have been going through PP's mind, for emitting a low keening sound that rose gradually to a high-pitched shriek, she rushed from the room and raced along the corridor, frightening to death several tourists who were on a 'Get

Acquainted with the Real Ireland' tour.

'It's only the banshee,' explained Ivy, who was trotting along in the wake of the deranged PP. 'Old Irish phenomenon. Occurs before the death of a member of certain families. It's a great mark of distinction — and the Pennefeathers are entitled to a banshee.'

'You mean, old Petunia is about to kick the bucket,' drawled a longhorn from Texas.

'Probably dying of a broken heart. Too sad she and Hiram H Hinkelheimer did the splits,' put in his wife.

'Oh, no!' Vicky, following behind, realised it was essential not to frighten away the cash customers; with lawsuits impending, every penny would be needed. 'It could be for an uncle or a greataunt or someone from across the sea. It's just a quaint old Irish custom.'

The tourists, mystified but reassured, passed on.

'Why didn't we think of that?' Vicky said to Tansy when they were back in their room. 'A couple of doses of a real live banshee and those tourists would have melted like snow in July.'

'I wonder what the next step is?' wondered Tansy.

'Don't worry. We'll hear about it soon enough,' answered Vicky. 'Good, there's the dinner-gong — I'm starving.'

9

More Disasters

A council of war was called for 3 pm in the Presidential Suite. When the children arrived, Ivy, who had passed up a second helping of ice-cream, had got there before them. Whatever she had been saying hadn't helped. PP was in a black mood, seething with rage.

There was a long, long silence.

'You'll have to get solicitors,' said Vicky. 'If you're going to fight the case.'

'Of course, we're going to fight the case,' snapped PP.

'Isn't it lucky you didn't get rid of the tourists?' said Ivy. 'Just think of all those bills thudding through the letterbox . . . and no money coming in. . . And you've no idea of what legal costs are these days! Senior barristers. Junior barristers. Briefs. Refreshers. Appeals. There's no end to it. Even if you win the case, you'll probably have to sell the castle to pay the legal costs.'

'I though the loser paid,' said Vicky.

'If she has any money,' simpered Ivy. 'And if Mrs. . .,' taking out her glasses and peering at the letter, 'Babblecock-Browne loses, she won't have any money, will she?'

'Why don't you ask Snivell, Snivell & Crouch for their opinion?' asked Joey helpfully.

'Can't. They've gone over to the enemy, hook, line and sinker.'

'Conflict of interests,' contributed Ivy.

'We'd better get another firm of solicitors,' said Vicky. 'I've looked up the Golden Pages. The nearest one is in Poreen ... Argue, Phibbs & Leech.'

'I've heard of them,' said Ivy. 'Old Phibbs used to be the *most* handsome man. And Leech has such a reputation ... never lets go. Sticks right in there.'

'Well, with a name like that he would, wouldn't he,' snapped PP.

'I'll make an appointment for the morning,' said Vicky.

'Tell them it's a fight to the death,' glowered PP.

'This,' said Furball to himself, 'is going to be one of those weeks.'

It was indeed one of those weeks.

Argue, Phibbs & Leech were anything but encouraging. Sounding as if they'd just swallowed a shelf of law books, they gave their collective opinion.

'Rights of the widow supersede all others. Two-thirds of the estate if deceased died intestate. Do let us see the so-called will, dear lady, so that we can judge if it was properly executed. If properly executed, widow entitled to one-third. See Judgement Cloak v Dagger, Scales v Waite, Holly v Iveagh...'

'... not forgetting Noone v Knight...'

'... and, of course, Hogg v Bacon...'

The legal eagles paused for breath.

'That's enough,' interrupted PP, tired of all this batting to and fro of the debris of people's lives. 'The point is, what are my chances?'

'Of holding on to everything? Not a chance. The only question is two-thirds or one-third.'

'But the will said...' croaked PP.

'Immaterial, dear lady, and largely irrelevant. Your

Greatuncle must have overlooked the Succession Act.'

'Probably never heard of it,' said Ivy prettily, batting her eyelids at old Phibbs.'

'Ignorance of the law is no excuse,' sniffed Phibbs, giving her a look that would have caused a Supreme Court Judge to quail.

'So I've no rights in law,' raged PP.

'I wouldn't quite put it like that,' Leech sounded pontifical. 'If the will is in order, you get two-thirds. Surely that's enough for you — a single lady, with no great expenses, one would imagine. Maybe the widow is struggling to bring up ten children — and you know what they cost! Probably even now at her wit's end to put bread on the table. Turning patched jackets for the third time. Awake all night worrying about the phone bills, the ESB, the mortgage repayments. Surely you wouldn't want to do the poor penniless widow and the orphans out of their teeny share?'

'It's unlikely the claimant will settle for less, but

you might try,' advised Leech.

'We'll do our best,' purred Phibbs, rising to indicate that the meeting was now at an end.

'Everyone is on her side,' said PP bitterly as they left.

A battleaxe of a secretary sidled up as they got to the front door. 'Perhaps you wouldn't mind giving us a few details.'

She handed PP a form with a list of questions which, if honestly filled in, would give them a blueprint on the life and hard times of the witch.

'They have to be *so* careful,' said Ivy as she put the car into reverse, narrowly missing two pedestrians and a butcher's boy. 'So many people rush into law and then find they can't pay the bills.'

'Keep your mind on the road,' hissed PP.

'Thank goodness we didn't get rid of the tourists,' whispered Tansy to Vicky.

'At least they'll pay for the court case,' answered Vicky grimly.

'Let's hope,' thought Furball, 'they haven't finally got the message.'

Descending for breakfast the next morning, Vicky and Tansy could hardly pick their way through the Fensi and Gucci suitcases and overnight bags that were cluttering up the Great Hall. It looked as if every guest in the castle was assembled there.

'What's happening?' asked Vicky of Philpot, who was only capable of wringing his hands and muttering, 'Disaster! Disaster!'

Tansy waylaid a passing shorthorn and asked winningly, 'Why is everyone leaving?'

He looked at her, stunned, then passed on, bleating.

'Honey, you're sure you packed the orthopaedic back-rest?'

'Fetch PP,' ordered Vicky as Joey appeared.

The witch came down in double-quick time, and viewed the milling throng with a marked lack of comprehension.

Clapping her hands for silence, she roared, 'Just what is going on?'

'We're leaving, Mam,' said an entrepreneur from Oskosh. 'Jes gotta leave.'

'What do you mean, got to leave? You're booked in for fourteen days minimum. No refunds. Besides,' with her most winning smile, 'today is the day for Today's Special. What is it, Vicky?'

'Duck à la Surprise?' supplied Vicky.

'What's the surprise?' asked Jassy.

'The duck,' said Vicky, from behind her hand.

The Duck à la Surprise didn't seem to cut much ice with the frantic throng who were all trying to get to the door, where the first of a fleet of buses had just appeared.

'And there's a marvellous gig tonight in the Dungeon Tavern,' continued PP, clutching a passing arm. 'The Chieftainesses, in a programme guaranteed to bring tears to the eyes. Or money back. Handkerchiefs supplied.

'Haven't you heard?' asked a Sheik as he billowed by. 'About the war?'

'War, what war?'

'Pet-oonia, dear,' gushed Ivy as she fought her way in through the front door and up to where PP and the children stood enclosed in this sea of activity. She had just been down to the village to buy the *Daily Dependent*, no copies having been delivered. 'Such dreadful news! It's war! That awful man, Soddom Hasten, has just declared war on the entire world!'

'But why does everyone have to leave?' raged PP. 'We're a million miles away from whatever his name is.'

'Lady,' said the last straggler, 'we're only a rocket launch away. We've just gotta get home.'

'How long has this been going on?' PP's voice echoed around the empty Great Hall. 'Why does nobody tell me anything?'

'But, of course, dear,' soothed Ivy. 'You were so engrossed in the forthcoming lawsuit ... and the widow ... and the ... Why, nobody has looked at a paper for days.'

'No tourists,' shouted PP. 'But we need the money. Who's going to pay Argue, Phibbs & Leech? I can just imagine the bills *they're* going to chalk up.'

She spoke with a bitterness that was not entirely due to the thought of all that cash on the hoof disappearing down the front avenue. Having thought about the solicitors' advice to make a settlement, she had written to Snivell, Snivell & Crouch, offering one third of the estate, divided thus:

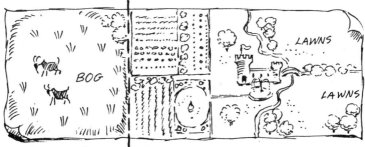

Her handsome offer had been contemptuously rejected in a curt note indicating that the widow had her mind on a bigger and better slice.

'Look!' PP felt a sudden tug on her sleeve. Joey was pointing at the door. 'They haven't all gone. The tourists I mean. Here's one just coming in.'

Coming through the door was a ravishing blonde, with a very large hat, very high heels and a very tight skirt. A taxi driver staggered in after her, carrying fourteen suitcases and a small dog. As she paused by the reception desk, PP and Hanratty almost fell over themselves rushing to greet her.

'So dee-lighted to welcome you,' PP could not have been more effusive.

'Do hope you enjoy your stay,' enjoined Hanratty.

'Do let us know if you have any special requirements,' gushed PP.

'What a charming little fellow!' enthused Hanratty as the dog almost took his thumb off.

'Perhaps you wouldn't mind signing the register... Just a formality.' As Philpot, bowing low, put the form before her, the gallant Hanratty intercepted it.

'Your name...'

'My name,' said the blonde, 'is Bibi Babblecock-Browne, wife of the late Fruzey Few-Browne, who was my dear, dear husband.'

'WIFE!' stuttered Philpot, aghast.

'Of ten years and three and a half days,' she said, burying herself with loud sobs, in a lace-edged handkerchief, before continuing, 'I'm here to claim my inheritance. I'm the rightful owner of Bashford Castle.'

The onlookers fell back in amazement. This was, literally, the last straw.

10

See You in Court

The Courtroom was hot and stuffy.

'I thought we were getting old Judge Pumperknickel.' Snivell Senior showed annoyance.

'Fell under a bus last evening,' supplied Snivell Junior. 'Substitute — Poppadum. Unfortunate — line of defence gone for a burton.' They had been relying on the baby-blue eyes of Bibi, and the harpy looks of PP.

'Open the windows,' barked the judge when he had been ushered in to the cry of 'Be Upstanding'.

He was a small fat man with a pair of maximum magnifying glasses. 'Can't see a yard,' grumbled Snivell Senior. 'What a turn-up!'

'I can't, your Honour,' croaked the clerk. 'They're stuck.'

'Disgraceful. Make a note of it. Unless these windows are unstuck by the time I am here again, I refuse to sit.'

'Why can't he stand?' queried Joey.

'Shssh...' responded Vicky. 'That's legalese.'

They were all sitting behind the bench where Argue, Phibbs & Leech were ensconced, PP under strict instructions not to open her mouth. Ivy had changed the flowers on her hat to yellow daffodils — symbol of hope.

Snivell Senior opened the case for the claimant, Bibi Babblecock-Browne. 'I ask you, my Lord, to look at this tragic figure before you, this poor penniless widow

cast forth upon the waters of the world, flotsam upon
the sea of life, tossed hither and thither mercilessly
by the winds of fortune, thrown aside like a discarded
rag, after a lifetime of dedicated service and selfless
devotion to an elderly monster, who,' here his voice
descended several octaves, 'can't have been the easiest
person in the world to live with. He had, I understand,'
directing a look of withering scorn at PP, 'some
Pennefeather blood in him. That speaks for. . .'

'Get along with it,' snapped Poppadum who had a
luncheon appointment at 1 pm, not to mention an
afternoon at the races.

Snivell Senior, not in the slightest disconcerted by
this interruption, expanded on his theme. 'Distraught
widow — poor as a church-mouse — taking in washing
— working her fingers to the bone — while others,'
another steely glance at the furious PP, 'take unlawful
possession of her rightful inheritance, waxing rich on
the proceeds thereof. . .

'It is not for me to pre-empt the line the defence
may take in this tawdry case. That will shortly be
outlined to you by my learned friend,' a bow to Argue,
Phibbs & Leech, 'and I have no doubt that they will
discharge their obligations in this distasteful case to
the best of their ability. . .'

'We are greatly obliged for the comments of our
learned friends,' responded Phibbs, bowing to Snivell,
Snivell & Crouch.

'Whose side are they on?' choked PP to Vicky. She
was about to give Leech a dig in the ribs when she
was restrained by Jassy.

'I get the picture,' grunted the judge. 'Unhappy
marriage. Unfeeling husband. Downtrodden wife.
Harpies of relations moving in and claiming everything.

Happens all the time...' He yawned, bored to tears. Then, remembering the races, he brought himself back to earth. 'Now, was there a will? Ah, yes, here it is... Well, it seems an open and shut case to me. I give judgement that...'

PP uttered a strangled cry and poked Leech. 'Don't we get to say anything?'

'What's the point? She's the wife and that's that. Mustn't antagonise him. He hates being argued with ... diverts him from his line of thought.'

'What's all the noise?' roared old Poppadum. 'Silence in court. As there are no arguments for the defence, I...'

Suddenly he paused, and said in a menacing voice, 'There's a cat in the Courtroom.'

'A cat?' The clerk turned pale, knowing his Lordship's aversion to anything on four legs.

'I distinctly saw a cat, under there,' pointing at the Argue, Phibbs & Leech bench. 'A wretched mangy little thing, full of fleas I'll be bound. GET THAT THING OUT OF HERE!'

'So this is Justice,' thought Tansy, her eyes round with wonder.

The trial was suspended while everyone searched everywhere. Luckily Furball had jumped into one of the witch's pockets in the nick of time.

'Blind as a bat,' grumbled the clerk, who, down on hands and knees, was searching the floor inch by inch. 'And always seeing things that aren't there.' Straightening up, he announced, 'The cat has gone, so please your Lordship.'

'And good riddance too,' grunted Poppadum. 'Now where were we...'

'My Lord,' said Vicky standing up. 'There is an unusual development. The defendant has instructed me to discharge her solicitors.'

A buzz of excitement ran through the whole Courthouse. People gathered in from other courts. This was High Drama.

'Most unusual,' agreed the judge. 'Who are you?'

'Victoria Ross-O'Brien. I'm taking over the defence. I ask that Argue, Phibbs & Leech be treated as hostile.'

The judge squinted in her direction. 'Who is instructing you?'

'My learned friend, Jasper ffrench-Fawcett of the well known legal firm of ffrench-Fawcett, Pollock & Tunney.'

'Sound very fishy to me,' said Snivell Senior, giving rise to that well known phenomenon 'Laughter in Court'. He had a weighty consultation with Snivell Junior as to whether they should point out to the judge that due to his being blind as a bat, he was allowing two unqualified persons to usurp the perogatives of their elders and betters, sully the great name of the Irish bar and degrade the noble professions of soliciting and barristering.

'Better not,' concluded Snivell Senior after mature reflection. 'You know how he gets if he's crossed. Things are running our way. Let the hare sit. What can two children do, after all? They're up against us, Snivell, Snivell & Crouch, the greatest legal brains in the country.'

It was probably the most unsound decision of his entire career. Could he have been privy to the last few days of frenzied effort by the children, he would not have dismissed the challenge so lightly. And the smile on his lips, so soon to disappear, would not have appeared at all.

Argue, Phibbs & Leech rose en masse, gathered up their books and papers, and saying, with one voice, 'We have never been so insulted in our entire lives,' left the Courthouse. Leech lingered behind just long enough to say ominously to PP, 'We'll be in touch.'

'If you think you're getting a penny out of me after that disgraceful performance, you've got another think coming.'

'Silence!' roared the judge. 'This case is getting out of hand.' Squinting down at Vicky, he snapped. 'Well, if you've got a point to make, make it and be quick. I've really come to the conclusion that...'

'I won't be two minutes, your Honour,' interrupted Vicky sweetly. 'I just have a few questions for Lady Few-Browne.'

'Don't call her that,' fumed PP.

Vicky crossed the room, with the confident manner

of a watcher of LA LAW, not to mention Rumpole.

'Now, Lady Few-Browne,' she said smoothly. 'You must have had a terrible life. As I listened to my learned friend here,' bowing at the still smiling Snivell, 'I thought how cruelly fate had treated you. It is surely no wonder that you have aged so much.'

'Aged?' Bibi sat up and put a hand to her blooming cheeks.

'Hard work and misery add on the years, don't they? But looking at you. . .'

'Get to the point,' interrupted the judge; the hands of the clock were coming perilously close to 12:30.

Snivell Senior, yawning, was preparing to pack up his files.

'I'm almost finished,' said Vicky. Turning to Bibi, she continued, 'It is amazing how young you look, considering what you have been through. Why, no one would ever take you for a woman of fifty plus. . .'

'Fifty plus!' breathed Bibi. 'What are you talking about? I'm only twenty-two — and I'm told, by my friends, that I look even younger. . .'

'Ah, twenty-two. So you must have married your late husband at the age of eleven.'

'But . . . but . . . but. . .'

Too late Snivell Senior saw the trap.

'Don't answer that question,' he flapped uselessly.

'Our case, my Lord,' said Vicky, 'is that the plaintiff was never married to Lord Few-Browne. How could she? She would only have been eleven at the time. Not only do we have her own admission that this is so, but,' and here Jassy produced a document, 'here is a copy of her birth certificate. . .'

'Case dismissed,' said old Poppadum, leaping to his feet.

'Be upstanding in court,' droned the clerk.

'Amazing!' said everyone.

PP's face was actually smiling. Tapping poor Bibi, who was still in floods of tears, she said, 'Don't worry, love. Come back to the castle and have a nice cup of tea — be sure to go round to the kitchen entrance! Attempted fraud is *so* exhausting...'

Back at Batsford, a notice had appeared in the Great Hall. They all gathered round to read it:

ANTIQUES ROADSHOW
Live tomorrow from Batsford Castle.
Featuring the Castle's fine collection
of oriental porcelain.
Hosted by Professor S Batty.
Bring all your antique bits and pieces —
and yourself — for valuations.

'What fun!' they all thought.

'That'll bring the tourists back again,' said PP happily. 'Now, champers everyone.'

As they sat around sipping champagne, Vicky and Jassy were the heroes of the hour.

'I really got the idea from Jassy,' said Vicky modestly. 'We were talking about Bibi and he said to me, "How could she be married for ten years ten years ago? My mum has been married for thirteen years and she looks years older than Bibi."

'Of course, I thought, that's the answer! She's far too young to have been married to someone who died ten years ago — we told Argue, Phibbs & Leech to follow that line of enquiry. Anyway, we thought the judge would be sure to suspect her. We were worried when old Poppadum came on and we realised he couldn't see a yard. But in the end that worked to our advantage; if he could have seen us we probably wouldn't have been able to take over the case.'

'These stupid solicitors,' chortled PP. 'All taken in by baby-blue eyes and long eyelashes ... Joey, supplies are running low. More champers...'

'This is the life,' said Ivy happily.

Tansy, who complained that the bubbles went up her nose, offered to go down to the cellar.

When she came back, she had a bottle of champagne in one hand and a strange mushroom in the other.

'Look at this,' she said, holding it out. 'I found it growing in the cellar.'

Petunia took one look at it, turned a paler shade of pale, and uttering just one word, 'Merulius,' in a hollow voice, fell prostrate to the ground.

The dreaded Merulius Lacrymans had struck again!

11

A Japanese Riddle

While the witch retired to bed with herbal tea and an ice-pack, Ivy explained all about Dry-Rot.

'The most *terrible* disaster that can befall a house ... mushrooms appearing everywhere ... floorboards crumbling ... threads of merulius leaping all over the place ... nowhere safe — and if it gets into the roof ... nothing for it but to dismantle the whole place...'

'Does it cost much to get rid of it?' asked Jassy.

'The earth ... and more,' was the comforting reply.

'Well, there's nothing we can do about it at the moment,' said Vicky. 'The experts will be here in the morning. Meanwhile, I'm going to go down and have a look at the roadshow.'

'Maybe that professor-whatever-his-name-is will find a treasure here,' said Joey. 'Then we'll be able to save the castle.'

'Some hope,' said Vicky sadly. 'You can't expect two miracles in one lifetime. But after fighting off Bibi, it seems such a shame we'll probably lose the castle anyway.'

But PP sat up excitedly when the children came to visit her en route to the roadshow.

'I do remember hearing that there was a great treasure at the castle. Philpot was even mumbling something about it the other night. Let's go and see.'

Down in the Great Hall the roadshow was in full swing. There were cameras mounted on mini scaffolding and a giant spotlight dazzled under a big umbrella. The Professor was being powdered, puffed and fussed over by the make-up ladies. A thin scrawny man with a tee-shirt labelled PRODUCER was shouting '5-4-3-2-1! Action!'

'We are here today,' began the Professor, 'at Batsford Castle, home of the late Lord Few-Browne — sea pirate, importer/exporter, Fine Art Collector Extraordinaire — to look at his fine collection of early Japanese porcelain. The china is, as you can see, rich, harmonious and free-style in decoration. The glaze is ... bla ... bla...'

'Look!' whispered Vicky. Two dear old ladies were struggling in through the door at the back, wrestling with a giant vase they had been admiring in the sun lounge. Plonking the piece in front of the bemused Professor, totally ignoring cameras, lights, producer and helpers, they asked sweetly if he could tell them where they could get one like it for their sitting-room, as the colour was *such* a good match for their curtains.

Composing himself as well as possible under the circumstances, the poor man tried to explain that there wasn't another like it. 'This vase,' he explained, 'dates from the 1660s. The quality is unmistakable. A truly remarkable piece. Although valuable in its own right, if part of a whole collection it would be priceless. It has been suggested that Lord Few-Browne did own a vast collection of early porcelain but since he passed on, no one has ever been able to find out if this was a fact ... or just hot air.'

'Let me say a few words,' said PP, deftly dislodging the two old dears and positioning herself in front of the cameras. 'Dear Lord Few-Browne was my Greatuncle and I inherited the castle from him. He loved riddles and puzzles and there has always been a tradition in our family that he hid this treasure and left a key to the place somewhere. Only where?' She batted her eyes at the Professor who edged around her to tell the thousands of viewers that all this was 'Interesting. Most interesting.'

'Of course,' continued PP, edging back before the camera. 'There's always the possibility that the old fox — if you'll excuse the reference — may have hocked the lot to cover expenses. Our family always had a penchant for cards and horses.'

The camera was now beginning to crowd in on Petunia. Still keeping her place in front of it and nattering away non-stop, she backed a few steps. On it came. She backed again, this time in more of a hurry.

'Stop!' yelled the Professor.

'Hold it,' shouted the petrified producer. 'That's a

valuable...' His mouth fell open. The witch, startled, backed right into the vase. All the poor man could do was wait for the crash.

'Aggh!' shouted everyone. The ones who couldn't bear to look closed their eyes. The others just gaped. Someone moaned, 'A priceless treasure gone forever.'

The producer's nerves were in such tatters that Hanratty insisted he go upstairs and lie down. The children started to collect the broken bits of china.

'Do you think it might be glued together?' wondered Joey.

'Look,' cried Tansy suddenly. 'Someone's dropped their purse.'

She pointed towards a small silk purse decorated with fire dragons, which was lying on the floor amid the debris. They crowded round her as she picked it up and examined it closely.

'It must have been inside the urn,' said Vicky excitedly.

'Quick! Open it!' urged the others, keen to see what it contained.

Alas! It was empty except for a bit of Japanese writing.

Jassy, imitating the Professor, held up the purse. 'Ah, yes ... a very fine piece ... used to keep money in! And we know that the Japanese were fond of spending money because there's none left ... ha ... ha!'

'I'll keep it anyway,' said Tansy who liked to collect all sorts of quaint old-fashioned things.

The Professor, who had been helping to pick up the pieces, suddenly came to life.

'Where did you find that, child?' he asked, pointing to the purse.

'I picked it up just now. It was in the urn. There's

nothing in it. But I thought I'd keep it because it looked so pretty.'

'*You* may have thought there was nothing in it,' said the Professor, 'but...' he examined it closely. 'Do you see these Japanese markings? They contain a message. I'll need my magnifying glass and if it's what I think it is... Hang on a mo...'

The producer was revived and the cameras rolled to record the historic scene for posterity.

Professor Batty finally cleared his throat, and began: 'It was a custom in ancient Japan to send messages in the form of a riddle from one potter to another. They did this to escape the wrath of the noble Nabeshima family who forbade the secrets of their kilns to be known outside the pottery.'

'I don't get it,' grumbled Joey aloud before he was hushed by Vicky.

'It's my humble opinion,' smiled the Professor, 'that

if we can decipher the riddle we will find the rest of the Japanese porcelain collection.'

PP, who had gone upstairs to adjust her make-up in case there was a chance of another television appearance, returned just then and grabbed the Professor.

'Tell me the riddle.'

The Professor began:

> *In my father's home there are many rooms,*
> *Harbouring many treasures,*
> *Awaiting glory in great tombs,*
> *Found only if warrior measures.*

Everyone fell into a stunned silence. Who would be the first to crack the code? Who would reveal the treasure? The producer was beside himself with joy. Next week's 'Roadshow' was guaranteed a capacity viewership. The discovery of a great treasure recorded on TV ... the tomb of Tutankhamen was nothing on it!

Time passed. Everyone was rushing here and there, and shortly, much to the annoyance of Philpot, the Great Hall began to look as if a ravening army had passed through it.

'I think I'm on to something,' quavered Ivy, rushing up to the Professor. 'Batty, dear boy, I think I'm on to something...'

She rushed to look behind a large hanging tapestry and cannoned into Joey, who was examining the wall, with such force that she sent him flying into a potted palm. He, in turn, crashed into Jassy who was giving the palm an in-depth inspection. Jassy teetered alarmingly before toppling heavily on to the suit of armour.

'That's right,' snapped the witch. 'Take the place apart while you're at it.'

She stuffed the suit of armour up against the wall. It fell down again immediately with an ear-splitting clatter sending Philpot two feet off the floor and causing him to turn puce.

'Dratted old thing,' muttered PP. 'Oh, keep your hair on, Peapot. I'll soon have it fixed.' Whipping off her trusty earring she began rescrewing it to the wall.

Just as she finished the last twist a loud rumbling was heard and a great stone moved backwards in the wall, leaving a great hole looking out and a bemused Petunia looking in.

'Quick, children!' shouted Professor Batty, legging it across the room to find a torch. 'I think Petunia may have found our treasure!'

He and the children held torches while Mr. Hanratty and Philpot took away more bricks, disclosing a room behind. It was full of large wooden crates. Reverently they carried them out into the Great Hall.

'It's like the tomb of...' said Ivy, wishing she had her *Guide to the 100 Best Antiquities* at hand.

'Better,' scoffed the producer. 'We've got it on film. Wait until the world sees this next week!'

When the crates were opened, they revealed the rest of the missing collection of porcelain — a collection that had never been seen in the modern world. The Professor was overcome — not only to see such beautiful works of art but to be present at a 'find' ... it was almost too much.

Everyone studied the riddle again. PP was nodding knowingly. 'Always knew it was somewhere round. Just waiting to be found.'

Tansy and the boys were still looking at the chart with the riddle written on it. They looked from it to the witch, and then back, as puzzled as ever.

'How did you figure it out?' they asked her.

'Oh, I err...' spluttered Petunia, not wanting to admit that she hadn't a clue — just when everyone thought she was the greatest brain in Ireland. She tried to look all mysterious and enigmatic.

Vicky, snapping her fingers, said quickly. 'I've figured it out!' Grabbing a red marker she wrote on the message:

In my father's house are many rooms, = the Castle
Harbouring many teasures, = the china collection
Awaiting glory in quiet tombs, = a hidden room
Found only if warrier measures, = the suit of armour.

'You see,' she explained triumphantly, 'if the suit of armour is properly screwed to the wall, it releases the entry stone to the room.'

'Exactly!' agreed PP in a knowing voice. 'Nothing to it really. We Pennefeathers were always very good at riddles.'

Clearing up all the debris, Philpot was muttering under his breath. No one, but no one, he moaned, had ever trained him to work under a boss like Ms Petunia Pennefeather. Nobody, but nobody, would believe that there was really somebody like her at large without being marked 'dangerous disaster' or 'deadly menace'. . .

Later that evening, Vicky found Ivy wandering around the Great Hall. She seemed to be having a fit of the vapours.

'Cheer up,' said Vicky helpfully. 'It's all been a bit of a strain. You'll feel better in the morning.'

'No, I won't feel better,' whined Ivy. 'Not as long as Puttyface Pennefeather owns a castle and I don't.'

'Quick,' said Vicky to Tansy. 'A bumper helping of ice-cream. On the double.'

When a consoled Ivy had been sent to bed, PP, the children and Furball took a walk by the light of the full moon. The castle looked splendid and the battlements cast long shadows on the lawns.

'Isn't it great the dry-rot isn't serious?' said Vicky. 'They say it's only an isolated break-out and hasn't travelled very far. So that won't cost very much.'

'And there's no sign of the death-watch. . .' Joey was beginning when Vicky kicked him. 'Don't anticipate disasters!'

Luckily the witch hadn't heard him so her good humour continued apace.

'All's well that ends well,' she chortled. She pointed

to the Pennefeather flag, and noticed for the first time the motto: 'Touch not the cat. . .'

'Where's the rest of it?' she exploded. There was silence. 'Oh well, come to think of it, nobody needs a glove to touch Furball.'

The little cat, trotting behind them, thought to himself, 'Just as well that bit was omitted. Otherwise, gloves would be the order of the day. . .'

'How lovely everything is!' whispered Vicky to Tansy and Joey and Jassy as they skipped along. 'Just what do you think is going to happen next? What could possibly happen next. . .?'

Suddenly Philpot emerged into view, proceding at a steady trot, indicating that something unusual was afoot, his usual gait being that of a rather slow snail. He carried a silver salver on which rested a telegram. As she had not got her specs with her, PP ordered him to read it aloud:

SAW YOU ON TV STOP BRILLIANT STOP SENSA-TIONAL STOP MAJOR PART IN NEW SOAP STOP FAX ACCEPTANCE HOLLYWOOD 999888776 INSTANT STOP FILMING STARTS MONDAY STOP YOURS HOPEFULLY STOP OTIS B

'Soap? What a hope!' chortled the witch. 'You all know my views on the dangers of over-washing the skin. I'm certainly not going to be fobbed off with *soap* commercials. In any case I couldn't, in all conscience, recommend a product I never use. What I want is a part with real meat in it.

'Dear Pet-oonia,' said Vicky in imitation of Ivy. 'You've got it all wrong. "Soap" means soap opera. Nothing to do with the stuff you don't use. Think

Dallas, Glenroe, Dynasty, Neighbours, Fair City, Home and Away ... why soaps might have been made for a talent like yours. You'll be a wow ... Philpot, go back at once and Fax acceptance. We leave for Hollywood on Monday.'

'Make it Tuesday,' said PP, difficult to the end. 'Must get cracking. Hair. Nails. Complexion. Figure. Exercises. Slimming.' She shot back to the castle, vowing never to go outside again without her skateboard. Not to mention her heated rollers and her 'lucky autographing' pen, etc, etc, etc.

'Hollywood! Wow!' said Jassy.

'Ivy is going to be as sick as a newt,' giggled Joey.

'Maybe they'll give us parts as well,' hoped Tansy.

'I'll insist on a walk-on part,' thought Furball. 'After all, I am on the Pennefeather coat of arms. Maybe a remake of Dick Whittington ...'

They all rushed back to the castle, leaving the moon in possession...

As to what happens next?

Further thrilling instalment on the way

TERRY HASSETT HENRY, LTCL, NCEA, has been teaching for fifteen years, covering all aspects of speech and drama, and is also involved in writing and producing material for school plays, pantomines, learning techniques. She works with children of all ages, and is currently concentrating on Montessori teaching for young children.

She now lives in Celbridge and is well known in libraries, schools and bookshops in the area for her 'witch' activities.

Her husband's name is Christopher and she has two daughters, Victoria and Chloe. Greatest ambition — to rid the world of dull gloomy books for children. *The Witch at Batsford Castle* is her second book; her first, also published by The Children's Press, was *The Witch who couldn't,* now out in a new edition.

TERRY MYLER trained at the National College of Art in Dublin, and also studied under her father, Seán O'Sullivan, RHA. She specialises in illustration and has done a lot of work for The Children's Press. Titles include *The Silent Sea, The Legend of the Golden Key, Cornelius Rabbit of Tang, Cornelius on Holidays, The Children of the Forge, Murtagh and the Vikings, Save the Unicorns,* and the two witch books. She lives in the Wicklow hills, with her husband, two dogs and a cat. She has one daughter.